PRAIS

"A pro at parodies." — The Associated Press

"The literary equivalent of a good *Saturday Night Live* skit." — *The Hollywood Reporter* on *Fifty Shames of Earl Grey*

"Witty... Clever..." — *USA Today* on *How to Survive a Sharknado and Other Unnatural Disasters*

"Fans of Carl Hiaasen's comic crime novels will have fun." — *Publishers Weekly* on *Hope Never Dies: An Obama Biden Mystery*

"Always funny." — LitReactor

ALSO BY ANDREW SHAFFER

FICTION

Ain't Got Time to Bleed

The Day of the Donald: Trump Trumps America!

Fifty Shames of Earl Grey: A Parody

Ghosts from Our Past

Hope Never Dies: An Obama/Biden Mystery

Hope Rides Again: An Obama/Biden Mystery

How to Survive a Sharknado

Secret Santa: A Horror for the Holidays Novel

The Telltale Hardon and Other Perversions

NONFICTION

Great Philosophers Who Failed at Love

Literary Rogues

POETRY

*It's Beginning to Look a Lot Like F*ck This*

Let's See Them Poems

Look Mom I'm a Poet (and So Is My Cat)

The Summer of '82: The Poetry of Brett Kavanaugh

CATSBY

This is a work of parody. The dialogue, thoughts, attitudes, and actions of its characters, even those based on public figures, are all fictional.

Cover design by Andrew Shaffer. Cover illustration licensed from Shutterstock.com.

Library Hardcover ISBN: 978-1949769074

Trade Paperback ISBN: 978-1949769241

Published by Dime House, a division of 8th Circle Entertainment (Louisville, KY) / Distributed by Ingram

First Dime House edition published January 2021

CATSBY

A PARODY OF F. SCOTT FITZGERALD'S THE GREAT GATSBY

ANDREW SHAFFER

What greater gift than the love of a cat?

— CHARLES DICKENS

CHAPTER ONE

In my younger and more innocent years, my father gave me some advice that's served me well: "Never rub another man's rhubarb."

No, wait—that was Jack Nicholson in *Batman*.

What was it my father told me? Oh, yeah: "Not everyone's had the advantages you've had in life, Dick. Unless you want to become a world-class asshole, you'll need to learn to check your privilege."

He explained that as an upper middle-class white male, I'd won the privilege lottery. We lived in a posh, gated community in the Chicago suburbs, free of crime and poverty. While this probably sounds idyllic to the modern reader, it was, in practice, very *boring*.

Don't get me wrong: My upbringing certainly had more ups than downs. I just sensed there was a more interesting world out there, one with conflict and drama. Growing up, I wasn't exposed to this other world through TV—my mother watched *Friends*, my father watched *Seinfeld*—or through the Internet, which was deemed too treacherous after my parents caught me ordering my own baby food on Amazon. It wasn't until I went to kindergarten that I realized just how much I was missing out on.

The school library's shelves were lined with thousands of novels, each a window into another world. Books were my escape from the prison of privilege. With books, I could be anyone, go anywhere, do anything. The book I remember being the biggest revelation was *The Adventures of Huckleberry Finn*. Although the school's copy was heavily bowdlerized, it was still quite a powerful tome. In the sanitized edition of Mark Twain's timeless tale, a boy befriends a stray orange tabby named Jim. Together, they boat down the mighty Mississippi.

Reader, I literally couldn't even.

We didn't own any pets, but oh how I longed for one! A dog or cat would have introduced a little excitement into our household. Alas, it was not meant to be. My mother hated dogs, because one had bitten her face off as a child. Cats were out of the question as well—my father was allergic to them. Every time he saw one, it would cause him to break out into obscenities and kick wildly at the poor creature. I once suggested he see a doctor for an antihistamine, and he started kicking at me. I guess he was allergic to children too.

But back to books. My love affair with the written word continued long past Huck Finn. In high school, I read all the classics: *Catcher In the Rye, To Kill a Mocking-*

bird, The Hunger Games Book Two: Catching Fire. When it came time for college, there was only one school on my short list: the University of Iowa, home to the venerable Writer's Workshop. I didn't want to write at the time, but in my mind the campus was a mecca for book lovers. My parents were understandably wary about sending their only son to a public university. At least I only wanted to read books, not write them! After I purposefully bombed my SATs—thus ensuring no Ivy League school would touch me with a hazing paddle—they relented.

During my first week on campus, I learned firsthand why Iowa had such a stellar reputation amongst writers: It was also one of the heaviest drinking schools in the country. It should come as no shock to the reader that I fell madly, wildly in love with alcohol. My four years passed by in a blur. The only thing I remember reading was the labels on my beer bottles.

When I moved back home, my parents asked if I had any plans for the rest of my life.

I did not.

They made it clear that a lot had changed in four years. It's like that old saying: You can't go home again, because your parents have become swingers and they've been using your bedroom for their bi-weekly key parties.

After some Googling, I discovered the only thing my English degree qualified me to do was work in publishing. My parents agreed to finance my East Coast excursion for a year, which I figured would be enough time for me to secure a real job as whatever it is people in publishing do. Based on my willingness to work without pay, one of the big New York publishers—Fandom House—hired me as an intern.

When the big day finally came, I hugged my father at the door. He handed me a rectangular white device about the size of a phone. The screen took up only a third of its face.

"It's a first-generation iPod," my father said. "They don't even make these anymore."

"For good reason," I mumbled. "What am I supposed to do with it?"

"It's for listening to music. I loaded it up with all of my favorite songs—there's a little Alicia Keys, some Train... When you have a kid someday, you add yours and pass it on. It'll be like a family heirloom."

I muttered a barely audible thanks. Perhaps I could find an antique store in the city and pawn it.

My mother embraced me next, crushing me with a powerful bear hug. "I'll...miss you...too," I choked out, coughing for oxygen. An x-ray would later reveal she'd cracked three of my ribs. Despite the pain, I would miss her. Who was going to cut the crust off my PB&J sandwiches?

Once I arrived in New York, however, I was too busy to miss the comforts of home. There were plenty of other things to occupy my time...other things like drinking. I wasn't alone in my love of alcohol. All of us drank too much. That was the tune of the times. These were the years just following the Great Recession, when the economy had begun to rebound. Just when you thought the stock market had hit a record high, along came another record day to blow it out of the water. The parties were bigger, the liquor cheaper, and the twerking looser.

The tempo of the city quickly wore me down. When I returned to the Midwest less than a year later, I was disgusted. Disgusted with myself, disgusted with everyone. There was only one person exempt from my disgust.

Or rather, one feline.

Jay Z. Catsby.

CHAPTER TWO

The history of my first and only summer in the city really begins the night I had dinner with my cousin and her husband Tucker Boobcannon.

Tucker and I were in a psychology course together our freshman year of college. I remember him leaning over my shoulder one day. We'd never talked before, but I knew he was a bit of a jock. I thought he was going to kiss me. It seemed like the sort of thing a macho man would do, at least in my mind. Instead of giving me a peck on my cheek, he started copying the answers off my exam. We were both busted for cheating and put on academic probation for a semester. He bought me a beer for causing me trouble, and—for reasons I still can't fathom—we became fast friends. I don't think he had many friends, to be honest, on account of him being something of a prick.

Miley was my first cousin. She was born and raised in Louisville, so I didn't see her that often until we both ended up at Iowa. I introduced her to Tucker one night, and before I knew it they were hooking up. Right there in front of me. It was an uncomfortable night.

After college, they moved to Park Slope. If you had money and children—both of which they had in terrifying abundance—it was undoubtedly the part of Brooklyn to be in. As I emerged from the subway, I marveled at how different the neighborhood looked from my own. I was renting a small beach house on the Jersey Shore. Even though they were only an hour's train ride apart, Brooklyn was light years ahead of New Jersey in terms of fashion and dining. In New Jersey, people were eating quinoa. In Brooklyn, people were wearing it.

I followed Apple Maps to the Boobcannons' address. Two hours on foot later, I found myself in Queens. I cursed the ghost of Steve Jobs. I settled into the backseat of a taxi in a pool of sweat. As we traveled back to Brooklyn, the little TV screen in the cab assaulted my senses with an endless loop of Jimmy Kimmel clips. Finally, just as I'd reached the point that I wanted to Kimmel myself, the car pulled to a stop.

I stepped out onto a beautiful tree-lined street. Row after row of charming, two-story townhouses extended in either direction as far as the eye could see. I rang the Boobcannons' doorbell. As I waited for an answer, my eyes drifted to their neighbor's house to the right. In the second story window, a curtain was drawn to one side. A furry figure clad in a maroon-and-black Star Trek uniform stared down at me. I raised my right hand and parted my fingers. The odd creature snapped the curtain closed without returning my Vulcan salute.

The door in front of me swung open. Tucker swallowed me in his arms with a giant bearhug. "Dick! How long has it been, old bro?"

"We graduated two months ago."

He set me down and gave me a wary look. "Too long, my bro. Too long!"

I followed him inside. "You have some interesting neighbors. The Star Trek fan next door...."

Tucker rolled his eyes. "Catrick Stewart?"

"Wait. That was *Sir* Catrick Stewart?"

"Is there another? Not only does he dress up all the time in that stupid cat costume, but he also wears that ugly leotard over it. We get dozens of nerds every day walking by, gawking at him and hoping to catch a glimpse of his royal highness. The sidewalk's just lousy with nerds at times."

"Sounds awful."

"Listen, Dick. I know you were always into books, but you were never a nerd. One of these days I'm going to go berserk and use my fists to beam one of these Trekkies straight to heaven."

"Are you complaining about nerds again, honey?" a woman called from the next room.

"Your cousin is here," Tucker shouted. Then, to me, "Miley's been dying to see you. Want a beer?"

I hesitated. I was twenty-one days sober—not by

choice, but by necessity. Since arriving out East, I'd done nothing but work, commute, and sleep. The few hours of free time I could find were usually spent reviewing manuscripts at home for my bosses at Fandom House. It was my first real job; if things didn't let up soon, I would throw in the towel and make it my last. I was lucky to find a few hours to sneak away to visit the Boobcannons. Did I want a beer? Absolutely. My big worry was that I'd fall back into the same pattern from college: one beer would turn into two, and two would turn into three hundred.

"I think I'm good," I said, declining Tucker's offer with a wave of my hand.

He recoiled in horror. "Dear lord. Who are you and what have you done with Dick Narroway?"

I sighed. "You know what? I'll take one. Just one."

"That's my boy," Tucker said, grinning. He ushered me into the living room, where he left me while he went to grab our beers. I glanced around the room; Miley was nowhere to be found.

A hand shot up over the couch, which faced away from me. "Is that my dear cousin, Dick Narroway? You're late, darling. So late."

"I'm still trying to find my way around the city," I said, peeking over the couch to find her stretched out. Miley wasn't alone. A tall, shapely brunette rolled off her and onto the floor.

"Whoopsie," the girl said, getting back to her feet.

Miley introduced us. "Dick, this is my bae, Cordon Bleu."

I shook Cordon's hand. Although this was our first meeting, I knew who she was—everyone did, in those days. Cordon Bleu was the reigning women's champion of competitive hot-dog eating. Not only had she won the women's title at the annual Statham's Hot Dog Eating Contest four years in a row, but last year she'd beaten the men's champ by downing more wieners than a cam girl trying to pay off her student loans.

"Nice to meet you, Ms. Bleu," I said.

Miley leapt off the couch and onto my back. My legs buckled out from under me, and she hit the floor with a thud.

I helped her to her feet. "How much have you two had to drink, Miley?"

She held her finger and thumb an inch apart and giggled.

"You never drank in college. What happened?"

"Kids, Dick. I have eight kids now. No—nine. I don't even know all their names. It's awful, so awful."

"You look great for giving birth to nine children," I said. For once, I wasn't lying to a woman. Miley still had the same thin waist she'd had just a few months ago. She had some bass (no treble), but didn't look like she'd given birth anytime recently.

"My nipples look like dog park chew toys. It's horrible."

"You're still breastfeeding? Should you be drinking?"

"She didn't give birth to the kids," Cordon said dismissively. "Her surrogates did."

"They were my eggs!"

"You're not even raising them," Tucker said, entering the room and handing me a glass boot filled with beer. "The nanny's doing all the work."

Miley shot her husband a nasty look, and he stuck his tongue out at her.

"Young love," Cordon said, flashing me a devilish smile.

I nodded, and sipped my beer. It was like drinking the piss of angels. Delicious. "You live around here?" I asked Cordon.

"Just in town for the summer. I'm a Chicago girl."

"So's Dick," Tucker said. "Except he has a penis. Not that that means anything these days."

"Chicago? That's fab," Cordon said.

"I assume you're competing in the hot dog contest next month?" I asked.

"I see my reputation proceeds me."

"Precedes," I corrected.

Cordon glared at me. I wasn't sure if she wanted to slap me or rip my cardigan off. I raised my eyebrows with a smirk, indicating I was game for either scenario.

"You said you're new to the city?" she asked. "Do you live in Brooklyn?"

I shook my head. "I work at a publishing house in Manhattan, but commute from the Jersey Shore. I heard that's where the best parties are."

"Is it true?"

I shrugged. "Haven't been to any yet. Work is killing me."

"I hear Catsby throws the sickest parties."

Miley broke away from her silent little battle with Tucker. "Catsby? What Catsby?"

Cordon spun around. "Why, Jay Z. Catsby. Is there any other?"

The color drained from Miley's face. Her husband felt her forehead with the back of his hand. "You feeling okay, sweetcakes?"

"Fine," she mumbled.

Cordon sighed. "Are we ever going to eat? I'm so hungry I could eat a horse."

"Do you want horse?" Tucker asked.

"Wait," I said. "They serve horse in Park Slope?"

Tucker crossed his arms. "I can get us a horse."

Cordon thought it over for a moment and then shook her head. "I can get that anytime back in Chicago. I want something fun. Something interesting."

"Cronuts!" Miley yelled, falling back onto the couch.

"No cronuts," Tucker said.

"Dossaints?" Miley asked.

"Now you're just making things up." Tucker pulled his phone out and began scrolling through his contacts.

Miley sat up. "Who are you calling?"

"The loony bin. I'm having you committed." Tucker turned to me. "Do you like chopped salad, Dick?"

"I like salad."

"I'm talking about *chopped* salad."

"What do you mean?"

"I mean they take a salad—all the ingredients like lettuce, and eggs, and tomato, and ham, and salad dressing—and they chop it all up for you."

I shook my head.

Miley looked at me incredulously. "You've never had?"

"I guess I've never had."

"But it's so marvelous, Dick! You know how sometimes you're eating a salad and you don't get every single ingredient in every single bite? Like, sometimes you get all lettuce and dressing, but no egg. Or no ham. It's just horrible. So horrible."

Tucker's eyes lit up. "Chopping the salad solves that problem. They take big knives and dice it into tiny pieces." He swung his hands through the air as if he was carving an enormous salad.

Miley nodded enthusiastically. "And in each bite, you get just the right amount of every ingredient."

I couldn't tell if they were putting me on or not. Cordon seemed bemused by the discussion. "So it's like someone else is chewing your food for you?" I asked.

Miley and Tucker glared at me as if I'd just called Taylor Swift a talentless hack.

"We're getting chopped salad for dinner, and then you'll see," Tucker said, putting the phone to his ear. "Yes, I'd like to place an order."

I turned to Cordon. "What about you? Have you ever had chopped salad?"

She shook her head. "I'm more of a tossed salad girl."

I narrowed my eyes. "Was that a..."

"Euphemism? You bet it was," she said with a wink.

What a filthy, disgusting woman.

I was in love.

CHAPTER THREE

We ate our chopped salad in silence until Tucker's phone buzzed in his pocket. He glanced at it under the table and excused himself.

A solitary tear rolled down Miley's cheek. "I'm getting another wine cooler," she said, excusing herself from the table.

Once she was gone, I turned to Cordon. "What do you suppose that was all about?"

"You don't know?" Cordon said, lowering her voice. "Dick's got a side chick in Williamsburg."

In the next room, I could see Tucker speaking into his phone in hushed tones, a broad smile on his face. "You think he's talking to her right now?"

"Didn't you see him snapping dick pics under the table during dinner?"

I shrugged. "That's just Tucker being Tucker."

"It's beyond rude."

I wasn't sure whether she was referring to dick pics or taking a booty call during dinner or some combination thereof. Before I could ask her for clarification, Miley returned, bottle in hand.

"How are you liking the chopped salad?" she asked me.

"I don't think I'll ever eat another salad unless it's chopped."

"Damn straight you won't, boy," Tucker said, returning. We all tried to avoid the bulge in his pants, which was eye level with me and too close for comfort.

"Can you sit down, honey? You're at half-mast," Miley asked her husband, shielding her eyes. Cordon also averted her gaze, pretending to be mesmerized by her chopped salad. Maybe she was; it really was as good as advertised.

Tucker, finally realizing his faux pas, sat down. He let out an exaggerated sigh. "Sorry about that, ladies. It's just when the blood rushes to my little head, I don't always think straight. You know what I'm talking about, Dick."

I shook my head violently.

"Or maybe you don't," Tucker said, glancing from me to Cordon and back with suspicion. "Say, Dick, why don't you tell Miley who you saw outside."

"Sir Catrick Stewart," I said, as if delivering news of a royal birth.

"Really," Cordon said.

"He lives next door," Miley explained. "Tucker, don't get started on the nerds."

"Who said I was going to start on the nerds? I was just making polite conversation with Dick."

"Once you get started, you won't shut up," Miley said. "You'll just make yourself angrier and angrier, and for no good reason."

"I'm sorry, but the neighborhood is lousy with them."

"What's wrong with nerds?" Cordon asked.

Tucker exhaled. "I'll tell you what's wrong with nerds. They're ruining this damn country. Used to be, they kept to themselves. They had their comic book conventions and their Star Trek gatherings and whatnot. Nowadays, they've taken over the whole damn world. You can't go to the movie theater without sitting through a half dozen trailers of comic-book movies. Superman and Batman I was fine with. Even Spider-man, I could handle. But Green Lantern?"

Cordon arched an eyebrow. "You at least liked *The Avengers*."

"Hated it," Tucker said. "Like I care about Scarlett Widow and Arrow Man. Don't get me started on that TV show, *Agents of S.H.I.T.* The only people who want to see these D-list super-heroes are nerds. They have too much disposable money. I suppose that was to be expected, since they mostly live in their parents' basements. There was a time when every other movie and TV show wasn't based on a comic book. There was a time when you could enjoy a movie without worrying about missing out on all the little in-jokes for these fanboys. Whatever happened to real movies like *Die Hard* and *Lethal Weapon?*"

"Shane Black directed *Iron Man 3*," I said.

Tucker stared daggers at me. "Who?"

"The director of *Lethal Weapon*," Cordon said, backing me up.

"I don't know anything about directors," Tucker muttered.

Miley stood up. "I'm going outside for a vape."

I joined her on the steps, if only to get away from under Tucker's oppressive presence.

"He's a bully," she said, pulling an e-cigarette out of her purse. Miley took a drag. The end of the stick glowed a cool blue. She looked as glamorous as a Kardashian.

"He means well," I said. "I think."

"You don't have to live with him. He gets worse every day."

"How are the kids?"

"What kids?"

"Your children?"

"Oh, those," she said with a little laugh. "I don't know, I haven't seen them this week. I guess the nanny would text me if something happens with any of them."

"They don't live here?"

She gave me a look like I'd just asked if testicles came in pairs.

"Do you have a favorite?" I asked cautiously.

"Tillie," she answered, perhaps too quickly. She

pulled a link up on her phone and handed it to me. "Here's a GIF of her."

The baby girl flailed in her crib like a turtle on its back. The GIF repeated, and repeated. I handed it back to Miley. "Cute," I lied.

"She's the only girl in the bunch."

"Eight boys, then?"

"Or nine? I don't know. But it was to be expected, with Tucker's sperm. He shoots straight testosterone."

The biology was suspect, but I had to admit it sounded like Tucker. "Well, with eight brothers, she'll certainly be well-equipped to handle men later on in life. She'll be smart. A girl's gotta be smart."

A pack of nerds in stumbled slowly by, their necks craned up toward Catrick Stewart's house. The windows were shut, and there was no hint of movement within. One girl in a green and yellow Loki hoodie held up her phone and snapped a picture of Stewart's home. Eventually, the nerds passed by.

"Listen, Dick—let me tell you what I said after I saw my daughter for the first time. Can I tell you?"

"Sounds reasonable."

"It'll go a little ways toward explaining to you how I feel about things these days. The first time I met our little Tillie, she was an hour old. I was exhausted from the labor, which had lasted forty-eight hours, but I just had to hold my baby for the first time right away. Our surrogate mother had just given birth and been sent home on the bus back to God knows where she was from. Alabama or Alaska. One of those A-states.

Anyway, the nurse handed my baby to me and she said, 'It's a girl.'"

"That's what nurses usually say in that situation."

Miley nodded. "But it wasn't the nurse who said it—it was Tillie. She was very bright for her age. Tucker didn't hear her, thank God. Who knows where he was or who he was screwing around with."

"Still, you should be proud. Tillie sounds like a smart girl."

"I hope not. I hope my daughter's an idiot. That's the best thing a girl can be in this world. An idiot."

"That doesn't sound very positive," I told her.

She blew out a cloud of scented mist. "It's not so bad. There are books for idiots nowadays."

"Like *Sex For Dummies*."

"Actually, I meant *Fifty Shades of Grey*."

I nodded sagely. I hadn't read the books, but then again I didn't have much free time to read for pleasure. My job at Fandom House kept me plenty busy. Still, I was familiar with the *Fifty Shades* books, because my bosses had assigned me to the "pull-to-publish" department.

If you're not familiar with that term, you're not alone: I had no idea what "pulling to publish" meant until my first day on the job. Apparently, *Fifty Shades of Grey* was originally published online as *Twilight* fanfiction. The story was set in an alternate universe where Edward Cullen was a rich businessman, not a vampire—little difference, if you ask me.

After E.L. James changed the names and published her trilogy to worldwide success, every publisher out there wanted a piece of the action. Acquisitions editors flocked to fanfiction websites in search of the next E.L. James, overturning rocks and watching the fanficcers scatter for cover. They snapped up as many fanfic stories as they could grab—a process known as "pulling to publish."

Once the writers signed the contracts, however, the editors realized there was a problem: Someone had to go through each story and change all the names so they couldn't be sued for trademark or copyright infringement.

This was easier said than done. You have to go through the entire manuscript and change not only the names but also other identifying characteristics such as eye color, skin tone, and even race. In *Fifty Shades of Grey*, the dark-skinned ethnic friend Jacob from *Twilight* was changed from a Native American to Latino, for instance. While that sounds as easy as using "find and replace," you actually have to read the story closely and change small details, like turning an Indian headdress into a sombrero. Naturally, the editors farmed the grunt work out to interns like me.

I didn't complain about the work because I knew I had to pay my dues. Plenty of eager young people gave up on their dreams when they found out how the sausage was made. I remembered that Miley had once had dreams about working in publishing, back when we were teens. That was before she met Tucker and decided money was more important than her silly dreams.

At least that's what I assumed. I couldn't see any other reason she was with Tucker. He was a hulking, brutal hulk of a brute who hadn't changed a bit since graduation. When a normal person gets worked up, their face flashes red with anger; when Tucker got mad, his skin flushed green like the Hulk. His biceps rippled beneath the tight arms of his Ralph Lauren polo shirt; his neck was thick as a tree trunk poking through his popped collar. He was obviously on some sort of performance-enhancing drugs. What he was training for, however, was a mystery. His days as a football lineman were behind him. I could only imagine what paranoid scenario he was planning for that would require a hedgefund manager to have biceps the size of the Rock's chest.

When Miley and I went back inside, we found Tucker and Cordon sitting on opposite sides of the living room couch. She had her iPad out, and was busy reading aloud to him the latest Internet articles on the topics of the day—the words, the opinions, the comments.

Oh, God, the comments!

We sat down and listened to Cordon read a Salon column calling for an end to the baby carrot holocaust. It seemed reasonably argued—and gave voice to the voiceless carrot parents who can't stand up the senseless reaping of generations of their children. But Cordon read a Slate column next, in which the author took the position that we should stop eating carrots altogether, regardless of their age. Not to be outdone, the Huffington Post ran a slideshow titled "The Vegetable Genocide You HAVE to SEE! (PHOTOS)." Miley began bawling uncontrollably after flicking through the HuffPo photos—whether she was paralyzed with fear or happiness, I've no idea. I took her breakdown as an opportunity to glance at the time on my phone. Already past ten. I stood and excused myself for the evening.

"Leaving so early?" Tucker asked, disappointment in his voice.

"But come," Cordon said. "We just passed the longest day of the year last week."

"It's been dark for hours," I pointed out. "I think the whole point of the long days is to take advantage of the daylight for as long as possible."

Miley perked up. "How many hours are in a day, Tucker? Twenty? Thirty?"

"I'm sure Dick knows. He's smart about these things."

"Well, I'm not a scientific man," I said. "If I had to guess, I'd say there's twenty-four hours in a day."

"And how many in a night?" Miley asked.

Cordon set her iPad down. "Does it matter? The night is young!"

"The night is young, but I am not," I said. I looked twenty-two, and was beginning to feel it as well. I had a decent buzz, but knew the longer I stayed the more I would drink. Skipping morning classes in college was tolerated and even expected; calling in with the brown bottle flu to work was frowned upon.

I returned to the Jersey Shore and sat on my back-door steps, marveling at the unending party on the beach just steps away. I closed my eyes and listened to the cracking of beer can tabs and crackling of bonfires, the rhythms emanating from the clubs, the mating calls of guidos and guidettes echoing through the streets.

I opened my eyes and took in the sights of the tanned, liminal bodies writhing and fist-pumping on the beach. The silhouette of a solitary figure crisply dressed in a three-piece suit caught my eye. The man stood at the end of a long dock, his right arm outstretched in the direction of New York City, groping at it as if it were a gigantic bosom on the horizon. I couldn't see anything in the distance besides a bright red light that danced and disappeared at odd fits.

After a spell, he strolled back down the dock toward the mansion where the sickest parties occurred every Friday and Saturday night. The moon didn't cast enough light onto him for me to make out his face. But just as he disappeared through the immense iron gate that separated his courtyard from the beach, I distinctly saw the flash of a tail.

CHAPTER FOUR

Tucker texted me the next day. He wanted to take me to lunch, to make up for practically shoving his junk in my face the previous night. I glanced at the manuscript on my computer. I was in the middle of a hundred-thousand-word novel about Edward Cullen as a chef, a common trope in the fanfic world known as "Chefward."

It was my third Chefward of the week.

"Meet you at noon," I texted back.

We met in the Fandom House lobby and he greeted me with another of his stiff bearhugs. "Sorry about last night."

I tried to tell him it was okay, that I'd enjoyed the chopped salad, but he would hear none of it.

"Miley was a drunk mess," he said. "I lost my temper. It's just...it's just the damn kids. Nobody ever told me that being a parent would be so stressful."

I nodded. I couldn't even begin to imagine the

responsibility of having kids at our age, even if you never saw them. "Where do you want to eat? There's a Chipotle just around the corner. Of course, since it's lunchtime, it will be packed."

He shook his head. "Chipotle, Dick? What are we, still in college? This is New York. We're going to Shake Shack out in Brooklyn."

"I think there's a Shake Shack a few blocks away, over on—"

"The one in Brooklyn is better," he snapped, cutting me off.

"I don't know. That sounds pretty far..."

"Nonsense," he said. "If I don't have you back in an hour, you can kick me in my baby-maker."

I didn't entirely trust him, but he knew the city better than I. We descended into the nearest subway station and caught a train to Penn Station, where we transferred to the L. I glanced nervously at the time on my cell phone. Twenty-five minutes had already passed since leaving Fandom House.

"Put that thing away," Tucker said. "Enjoy the ride."

I stashed my phone and leaned back in the hard plastic seat. The train was deserted except for a few poor, homeless souls. Above the gray walls and spasms of bleak humanity hung a colorful ad featuring a middle-aged man in a white lab coat.

"Having clear, beautiful skin has never been easier," the man—a certain "Dr. Zeckleburg M.D."—proclaimed. "Only takes a few minutes to apply. Approved!" Dr. Zeckleburg's drooping, darkened eyes peered down on me from the faded advertisement, brooding over the solemn dumping ground that was the New York City subway system. I looked sideways at an elderly woman several seats over. Her eyes were closed. I wondered if she was asleep or dead. New York was indeed a very different place than back home.

I ran my fingers over my own cheeks, which broke out occasionally. Did I need "tighter, firmer, younger looking skin" badly enough to undergo a "non-surgical THERMAGE procedure"?

Tucker jumped up as the train screeched to a halt. "This is our stop."

He was out the door before I could question him. I looked out the window at the station name. Bedford Avenue. I bolted after Tucker and caught up to him sprinting up the stairs. We emerged from the subway. We were in Brooklyn, but this wasn't his posh Park Slope neighborhood. There were too many flannel shirts, too many beards, too many vinyl shops.

"Where are we?" I asked as we passed an artisanal pencil-sharpener.

"Williamsburg," Tucker said.

"How far is the Shake Shack?"

"I don't know," he admitted.

I pulled my phone out. "I'll look it up—"

Tucker snarled at me. "Real men don't use maps."

"I was going to check Yelp."

"Forget it," he said. "Lima will know where it's at."

"Who's Lima?"

"My girlfriend. She works at a bookstore just around the corner."

So Cordon had been right about Tucker. In college, he hadn't always been the most faithful to Miley. Then again, it was college.

"Still sowing your wild oats, eh?" I teased.

He held up his ring finger to show off his wedding band. "Don't be crude, Dick. I'm a married man now."

I breathed a sigh of relief. "So you're not sleeping with this girl."

"Of course I'm sleeping with her. I'm just not spilling my seed everywhere. No more random hookups. I've settled down. I'm a one-woman man." He paused. "Unless you count my wife, in which case I'm a two-woman man."

He'd matured so much since Iowa. He was no longer a boy—he was a man. As I'd learned in my literary fiction courses, there was nothing more grown-up than having an affair.

We stopped in front of a little shop called Books and More. Tucker held the door open for me. I'd been in plenty of bookstores. This one didn't strike me as odd until I saw that they only carried paper books. How they stayed in business, I have no idea. The only bookstores left in the Midwest carried tablet computers, e-readers, board games, and plush toys.

The gentleman behind the counter surveyed us, one eye squinting and the other wide behind a thick-rimmed monocle. With his pencil-thin pornstache and faux-vintage Ms. Pac-man shirt, he could have been any one of a hundred hipsters in Williamsburg.

"Heya, Harper. Your wife around?" Tucker asked.

The man nodded toward the back of the store. "In the backroom. We just bought a collection of Choose Your Own Adventure books. She's sorting through them. We might have a complete set."

"I loved those books as a kid," I said.

Tucker scowled at me. His temper was really getting out of control. If anyone should have been pissed off, it should have been me. I was the one playing hooky from work as we hopscotched through the boroughs in search of nookie.

On our way to the back room, a black cat brushed up against Tucker's leg, nearly tripping him. "Watch where you're going, you stupid thing," he said, stomping at it. The cat darted off with a yelp.

"My father was allergic to cats too," I said.

He stared hard at me. "When we first bought our place, Miley wanted to get a cat. I don't know what she was thinking. Everyone knows I'm a dog person. I told her there's only one type of pussy I'll ever let in my house."

"What type is that?"

He shook his head. "Jesus, Dick, for such a bright guy you can be denser than a seventies bush sometimes." He knocked on the backroom door, and it swung open.

A woman was pawing through a box of the small

paperbacks. "Yeah?" she said, not bothering to turn around.

"Miss me?" Tucker asked.

The woman spun her head around and jumped to her feet. She threw her tattooed arms around Tucker and kissed him. I looked nervously over my shoulder, wary of her husband. Neither of them seemed to be the least bit concerned, and he was out of their line of sight. Still, it made me uneasy. I was used to conducting my affairs with a modicum of secrecy. That was all part of the fun of cheating, wasn't it?

"Who's this handsome fella?" she asked, eyeing me.

"This here is Dick, an old college friend."

"We just graduated two months ago," I told her, holding my hand out.

She bypassed my outstretched arm and hugged me. She smelled of old books and patchouli, with just a hint of irony.

"Dick, this is Lima Bean. She co-owns the bookstore with her husband—the clueless nerd you met up front."

She nodded. "So what are you doing here, Tucker?"

"We're looking to party," he said. "Why don't you put down these dusty old books and come along with us. We've got the afternoon free. We can head to the usual spot."

My eyes widened. Party? At one in the afternoon on a weekday?

"Sounds cool," she said. "Can we get cupcakes and Vitamin Water?"

"Of course. You think you can invite your sister, Molly?"

Lima giggled. "I'll see what I can do. You two head out, I'll meet you out front in a few."

On our way past the register, Tucker smiled and waved to Harper. "I'll see you later…after I do unspeakably filthy things to your wife."

Harper nodded absentmindedly and returned to his computer. I could feel my eyes bug out. What the hell was Tucker thinking, saying that to the girl's husband? Once outside, I hit Tucker in the upper arm and felt my knuckles turn to dust. It was like hitting a concrete wall.

"Jesus. What kind of supplements are you taking?" I screamed, shaking my hand out.

"Averbol, Dianabol, Danabol, Noreandrosterone, Stanozolol…plus the usual stuff, like testosterone, HGH. A little EGH."

"EGH?"

"Equine growth hormone. Need a hookup?"

Before I could answer, Lima joined us, a rubber horse mask covering her face. She gave us the thumbs up.

I glared at Tucker. "We're not going to Shake Shack, are we?"

He grinned. "We're going someplace even better: the Love Shack."

CHAPTER FIVE

The Love Shack was a hotel that Tucker liked to take his mistress to, since his wife would probably nag him if he brought her home. I agreed that he being discrete was the sensible thing to do, at least if he wanted to keep his *huevos* intact.

"Now, you're not to say a word of this to Miley," he whispered as we walked. "Bros before hoes."

Could I lie to my cousin? I didn't honestly know. I'd lied to plenty of women, usually ones I was dating. Still, I would try. For Tucker.

"You have my word," I told him. "Balls before molls."

"What are you boys jawing about?" Lima asked, removing her horse mask and racing to catch up to us.

"Just talking about man things, baby," Tucker said, putting an arm around her and taking the mask. "Like pick-up trucks, football, and Adam Sandler movies."

She wrinkled her nose. "Ewww."

Lima stopped dead in her tracks. Not that she literally dead, or that she was following tracks—I guess just saying "stop" would have worked, wouldn't it? Lima stopped. I followed her gaze to a pet store. Christ. Lima raced to the window and cooed over a litter of white Labs like she'd never seen a freaking puppy before.

"Can we go in?" she begged Tucker, pleading with puppy dog eyes. Combined with all the actual puppy-dog eyes in the window, it was enough to make any man break down. Tucker was overpowered, and he knew it.

"Fine, make it quick," he muttered.

I declined to follow Lima and Tucker inside. Pet stores have always held a particular sadness for me, since my family's house was a no-pet zone. I checked the time on my phone again. Going back to work was out of the question. Getting a few extra hours in on Saturday looked like the only way I was going to make up the time. I checked my Twitter feed, then my Facebook, then Instagram, then Tumblr, then Twitter, then Facebook, then Instagram, then Tumblr, then Twitter, then Facebook, then Instagram, then Tumblr, then Twitter, then—

Lima burst out of the pet store, an animal carrier in her clutches. Tucker followed her, a frown on his face and the horse mask under his arm.

"I've just always wanted one," Lima said.

"I'm not taking him home—Miley will kill me," Tucker said.

"You buy a little doggy?" I asked, peeking into the cage.

Before Lima could answer, a six-foot burst of flame shot past me, knocking me off my feet. I picked myself up off the pavement and marveled at the newspaper rack behind me in flames. People continued to walk by, as if nothing had happened—this was New York, after all. Nobody had time for a little street fire.

"It's a baby dragon," Lima said, smiling.

"Is that even legal?"

Tucker scoffed at me. "Listen to you. What happened to the Dick I knew back in college?"

"I think he'd be just as alarmed that there's a dangerous exotic animal in that cage."

Lima clutched the cage tight. "That's no way to talk about Judi Dench."

"That doesn't sound like a very appropriate pet name," I said.

"She's a classy dame," Lima said.

I followed them a few more blocks until we reached a rundown flophouse straight out of a gangster flick. The windows were boarded, the tin roof rusted. A sign posted on the door gave us warning: STAY AWAY FOOLS.

"Looks like your hotel's been closed for a while," I said. "Now can we go find something to eat? I'm so hungry I could eat at Subway."

"Nonsense," Tucker said, rapping on the door. "We stayed here just last week."

The door swung open, and a junkie who looked like

a *Walking Dead* cast member stumbled out. "Any bags today?"

"No, we don't have any bags of smack," I said, brushing him away with the back of my hand. "Let's get out of here before we step on a needle and get AIDS."

Tucker grabbed my hand. "You don't get AIDS from needles, you get HIV. And besides, a little respect—this man is the bellhop."

I looked closer at the bum and his tattered, loose-fitting clothes hanging off his gaunt frame. Upon further inspection, the scabs on his face were nothing more than theatrical makeup. "Welcome to the Love Shack," he said grimly, "the finest boutique hotel this side of the East River."

He ushered us inside. The lobby smelled worse than a Danny McBride egg fart. I stepped in a wet spot—wet with what, I couldn't say, because I wiped my shoe off on a passed-out wino and dropped a dollar on him as a tip. Maybe he worked at the hotel; maybe he didn't. Who was to say?

As Tucker was checking us in at the front desk, he turned to me. "Hutchence or Houston?"

"What?"

"Every room here is modeled after a famous celebrity hotel death. The only two rooms they have open are the Michael Hutchence and Whitney Houston suites."

I thought about it for a moment. Neither choice

sounded appealing. I just wasn't that big of a music fan, I guess. "What about Belushi?"

Tucker frowned. "You're kidding, right? You have to reserve that months in advance."

"Let's go with the Hutchence, then," I said, disappointment in my voice.

The third-floor suite was indeed as filthy and disturbing as the rest of the hotel, complete with a bloodstained mattress. I pulled my phone out and ordered delivery from the nearest Chinese restaurant I could find on Yelp. I needed to find something to eat, and fast. I don't think I'd ever gone more than eight hours without food in my life. I was beginning to feel lightheaded, like how poor people must feel all the time.

I peered out the window and onto the street below. I fantasized about leaving the sordid hotel room for the outside world, and walking until I found a park to sit in and watch Mother Nature dim her lights on Brooklyn. Every time I tried to leave in my mind, however, something pulled me back into the hotel, as if with ropes. I was at once within and without, both ensorcelled and revolted by the inexhaustible choices that the city offered.

"Oh, yessss! Oh, God yessss!"

I whipped my head around and caught sight of Lima's legs wrapped around Tucker's bare ass. I looked away before I saw any more. "I'm going to the bathroom and cry," I said to no one in particular.

Turns out the restroom was really quite luxurious compared to the dilapidated state of the rest of the hotel room, based solely on the fact that there wasn't any free-standing vomit in the sink or tub. I couldn't sit on the toilet seat, however—there was just no way. Instead, I removed the top of the tank and climbed up on it. While I was leaving an upper decker, there was a knock at the door. Before I could answer, Tucker swung the door open. He had a stained sheet wrapped around his waist, and frowned when he spied me perched above the tank.

"Can I help you?" I asked.

"Did you order food? There's a delivery man at the door."

"I'll be right out. I'm making room for it."

"Take your time. Lima is banging the delivery guy right now," Tucker said, shutting the door.

By the time I emerged from the restroom, the delivery guy had come and gone (and come and gone) and a coterie of hipsters had arrived. I counted ten. There were more packed into the room, but I only had ten fingers to count them on. People in publishing aren't great at math.

"What were you doing, giving birth in there?" Tucker asked, now wearing the bedsheet like a toga. "You've been gone almost two hours."

"I was tweeting," I said.

Tucker shook his head. "That's more embarrassing than dropping a deuce the size of Queens. Anyway, some of Lima's friends have joined us."

A gorgeous redhead sidled up to me. "I hear you're

from the Shore."

"I, uh, I'm renting a place on the beach."

The siren licked her luscious lips. "I was at a party there last weekend, at Catsby's."

I nodded. "That's what I keep hearing. I haven't met him yet."

Lima, who was milling about in Hello Kitty flannel PJs, held a palm out to me with a round, white tablet. "Have you met my sister Molly?"

I took the pill and swallowed it. I had been on MDMA just twice in my life, and the second time was that afternoon. The first time was a crazy night in college when I'd lost my virginity to an oak tree.

"A little party never killed anybody, right?" Lima asked, giggling.

"Except for, you know, all the celebrities this hotel's rooms are named after," I said.

Tucker grunted. "Why you gotta be so morbid, Dick? We're here to have fun. We're gonna be up all night to get lucky."

A hand reached around me and started unbuckling my belt. I turned to see a girl I'd never met before, a wicked smile on her face and pupils dilated to the size of basketballs. "What do you say, Dick?" she asked, slipping my belt off.

Not only would I not be returning to work that afternoon, but there was also a good chance now that I wouldn't return until Monday.

Eff it. YOLO, bitches.

CHAPTER SIX

Before I'd even cracked an eye open the next morning, I knew it was going to be a rude awakening. I was naked in a tubful of ice. There was also something on top of me, something warm and breathing...and not a woman, like I'd hoped. At least not a human woman. Lima's baby dragon was resting on my bare chest, snoring.

The previous night was a blur. A glorious, drug-fueled blur. I moved the dragon onto the floor. I was worried about it waking and searing my face off, but she didn't wake. Poor thing must have been as exhausted as I was.

As I sat up in the tub, I winced. My lower back was killing me. Of course it was—I'd slept the night away in a freaking tub. I stretched my arms and yawned. In the mirror, I caught sight of myself. It wasn't pretty. The right side of my flank was bruised something nasty. I touched my abdomen and nearly passed out from the pain. I turned around to examine my back in the mirror, and that's when I noticed the six-inch row of stitches.

Someone had stolen one of my kidneys.

I picked my clothes up off the floor and dressed. Thankfully, the kidney thief hadn't taken my most prized possession, as my phone was still in the pocket of my khakis. I checked it. No messages. More disturbing, however, was the time: 7:30 AM. *Saturday*. That meant I'd been asleep more than twenty-four hours. I'd missed work. Of course. What else had I expected to happen, hanging around with Tucker? He'd partied hard in college, and being a parent hadn't slowed him down any.

I tiptoed out of the bathroom. The hotel room was empty. There was a knock at the door. "Housekeeping," came a woman's muffled voice. It didn't seem possible that such a seedy hotel needed a housekeeper, but I opened the door anyway. I wasn't going to be sticking around much longer. I had to get to a home and see if there was any sign of my kidney. It was always possible that I'd just left it there before this whole drug-fueled adventure.

"I come back," the elderly woman said in broken English.

"It's okay, I'm checking out," I said, letting her in. She propped the door open, and I exited.

I was halfway down the hallway when she cried out behind me. "Wait!"

I stopped. Had she discovered my upper-decker already? "I'm sorry, I—"

"You forget your dog," she said, holding the door open as the baby dragon trotted past her, swinging its tail.

"It's not mine. It's—"

The dragon looked up at me forlornly. She had apparently formed some sort of attachment to me during the night. What had Lima planned to do with her, anyway? A fire-breathing dragon inside a warehouse of dead-tree books seemed like a bad idea. And Tucker couldn't take it in. How would he explain it to my cousin? Leaving the dragon at the hotel was out of the question, because it would probably end up in a shelter. I really had no choice. I returned to the room and found the dragon's carrier, and got on my knees to coax her into it. Judi Dench crawled into the cage willingly like a submissive little gimp.

I stopped. Had she discovered my upper-decker already? "I'm sorry, I—"

"You forgot your dog," she said, holding the door open as the baby dragon trotted past her, swishing its tail.

"It's not mine, it's—"

The dragon looked up at me forlornly. She had apparently formed some sort of attachment to me during the night. What had Lana planned to do with her, anyway? A fire-breathing dragon inside a warehouse full of [illegible] tree books seemed like a bad idea. And Tucker couldn't take it. How would he explain it to my cousin? Leaving the dragon at the hotel was out of the question, because it would probably end up in a shelter. I really had no choice. I returned to the room and found the dragon's carrier, and got on my knees to coax her inside. Dench crawled into the cage willingly like a submissive little puppy.

CHAPTER SEVEN

Once I arrived back at my beach house, I let Judi Dench out. She flapped her tiny wings. For a split second, I wondered if there wasn't a chance I might be able to keep her. My lease didn't allow for any pets besides cats. Unfortunately, there didn't appear to be a way to disguise Judi Dench as a kitty, even if I taped down her wings and had her fitted with a costume. There was another problem: She could breathe fire. I ordered a couple of DVDs online about dragon training, and prayed they would arrive before she spit another fireball at me.

Judi Dench let out a plaintive cry. I opened the door to let her outside, but she just stared back up at me. Maybe she was hungry. I assumed that I was starving too, but wasn't sure. I felt weak—but that could have just as easily been the fact that I'd recently undergone major, involuntary surgery. I opened the fridge. It was bare except for the bachelor pad staples: eggs, ketchup, and liquid eggbeaters. No wonder my gas had been getting steadily worse over the summer.

The doorbell rang, startling me. "Stay out of sight," I told the dragon. "I'll be right back."

I opened the door to find a well-dressed older gentleman who resembled Morgan Freeman, right down to the smug, all-knowing smile. "Can I help you?" I asked.

"I've brought you an invitation from my employer," he said, presenting me with a cream-colored envelope and a small, giftwrapped box. "An invitation...and a gift."

I set the box down on the side table and examined the envelope. "Dick Narroway" was written in calligraphy on the front. The back was sealed with red wax, and imprinted into the wax was a large paw print.

"Who is your employer?"

"Why, Mr. Catsby of course," the man said with a thin smile. "He lives right next door."

Finally, the pieces began falling together. I should have realized it sooner. The mysterious, well-dressed man with the tail on the dock was none other than the legendary Jay Z. Catsby! You probably already suspected this, because of the book's title. At least I hope you suspected it. If not, I'm a little worried about you.

"You're his butler?" I asked.

"Butler? That's such an antiquated term. I prefer to be called his bitch."

"Really?"

"No, not really. Of course I'm his goddamn butler. Good day, Mr. Narroway."

I watched the man leave through the bushes that separated our properties. He stumbled in the roses, and then disappeared into Catsby's yard.

I opened the envelope. Inside was a card. On the front, there was a vintage black-and-white photograph of a man's naked butt with a trumpet sticking out of the crack.

Dear Mr. Narroway,

You are cordially invited to my party this evening at 7pm. No need to RSVP.

Yours,

Jay Z. Catsby

P.S. Here's a belated "welcome to the neighborhood" gift. Enjoy!

I had stayed up some nights editing fanfic on my porch and listening to the sounds of men and women partying over the bushes, wondering just what one had to do to get an invite. I would have blown a grizzly bear. I didn't, and I'm probably a better man for not going to such extremes—a more alive man, at least.

I tore into the wrapping paper, revealing a cardboard gift box. The whole thing weighed only a pound or two.

Had he baked me something? A fruitcake, perhaps? I removed the lid...and found the corpse of a tiny mouse inside.

"I found some dinner for you, Judi Dench," I shouted.

CHAPTER EIGHT

Around nine in the evening, I threw a tuxedo jacket on over a dress shirt and jeans and snuck through the hedge. The party was already well underway. Not only had the dubstep been pounding since three in the afternoon, but the line of cars dropping pretty young things off at the front door was now backed up traffic a half-mile, all the way past Bruce Springsteen's place.

Judi Dench was in the carrier on my back porch, where I hoped she'd sleep the night away. There wasn't much to set ablaze on my porch, except for the giant pile of firewood and the hundreds of stacked copies of old newspapers.

Oh, and I still hadn't found my missing kidney.

"Excuse me, waiter," I said, approaching an older man in a white suit. "Do you know where I might be able to find the lord of the manor?"

The waiter scowled at me. "I'm not a waiter—I'm the writer Tom Wolfe."

I apologized and moved through the crowd toward the house. The name was vaguely familiar, but all of the old white male writers sort of blended together for me. Tom Wolfe, Philip Roth, Margaret Atwood.

There was a tap on my shoulder. I swung around and found myself face-to-face with Cordon Bleu. "Having fun yet, stranger?" she asked.

"Nice to see you," I said. "Still training for your big competition next week?"

"Like you wouldn't believe. I'm taking the night off from wieners. Just champagne for me tonight." She sipped from the flute in her hand.

I could feel the stitches acting up again. "Do they have anything harder?"

She shrugged. "Harder than champagne? You want to kill your liver?"

"Is the liver anywhere near the kidneys?"

"How should I know, Dick? I'm a competitive hot-dog eater, not a doctor." She shook her head. "You feeling okay?"

"Long story. I'm not staying long. I just got this invitation from Mr. Catsby—"

"An invitation! No one gets an invitation to a Catsby party."

"I did."

"How odd," she said, leading me inside the mansion. "I believe you, but it's very strange."

"Have you met him?"

"Who? Catsby?" She laughed. "Don't be absurd. No one's met him. He's like bigfoot."

"So he's really hairy and walks funny."

She shook her head. "I meant he's mysterious and he craps in the woods."

I glanced around at the assembled throng of guests, chatting and drinking and dancing in three-dimensional splendor. A Kanye West track was thumping so hard that my teeth were shaking in their sockets. It had been a while since I'd had a dental checkup, maybe that was something I needed to get checked.

We found the kegs, and a waiter handed me a Solo cup and a Sharpie.

"Let me guess, you're not a waiter—you're some fashionable writer," I said, taking note of the gentleman's thick-rimmed glasses and bookish demeanor.

"I'm a novelist. The name's Jonathan Safran Foer," he said. "But I'm also a waiter."

"Oh," I said, avoiding his plaintive, sadding gaze.

I scribbled a crude penis on my cup. Cordon scrunched her face up in mock offense.

"Dick," I explained. "It's my name, and this is how I sign things. With a little drawing of a—"

"—dick," she said, and we both laughed. God, I loved this woman.

I pumped my cup full of Miller Lite and took a swig. The beer was cool and refreshing, and the same golden color going down that it would be coming out. If my remaining kidney did its job.

"I've been drinking for the past week," Cordon said.

"How about we find someplace quiet to sit down for a bit?"

"Like a library?" I teased.

"I think that's on the third floor," she deadpanned.

We wandered through the vast interior of the mansion—through the living room, through the dining room, through the bowling alley.

"So who is this Jay Z. Catsby?" I asked Cordon as we passed through a long, cavernous hallway lined with old black and white photos. Upon closer inspection, they appeared to be recent Instagrams, printed out and framed.

"Who is Catsby?" Cordon asked. "I heard he killed a man. I heard he's a member of the Illuminati. I heard he's Hugh Jackman's butt double."

"Why don't we just find him and ask? He's got to be here somewhere."

Cordon peeked into a room and waved me through. We'd found the library. So she hadn't been kidding. There were hundreds, if not thousands, of printed books in the room, all organized on shelves according to the Dewey Decimal system. This was a proper library, right down to the row of computers in the middle of the room, where old men clicked on pornographic websites, pants unzipped.

"Who cares who he is?" Cordon said. "He throws large parties...and I like large parties."

"You like large things?" I asked suggestively.

Cordon slapped me on the arm. "You're so dirty, Dick."

A woman our age with her hair in a bun put a finger to her lips and shushed us, pointing at a sign. "Welcome to the Catsby branch of the Jersey Shore Public Library," it read. "Quiet, please."

Cordon lowered her voice. "It's so rare that a woman runs across a man who can say filthy things and not sound infantile."

I farted, and we both doubled over in laughter.

Unfortunately, I laughed so hard that my stitches tore asunder, sending me to the ground in a screaming fit of pain. This no doubt threw the librarian into further paroxysms, but what else could I do? I was bleeding to death on the floor of Catsby's library amidst a pool of light beer. A good death, but a death nonetheless.

CHAPTER NINE

"Having a good time, Old Spice?"

I opened my eyes slowly. I'd been moved from the library and was resting on a hospital bed. Someone was leaning over me. As his face came into focus, I realized I was being attended to by an enormous talking cat. Cordon Bleu hovered over his shoulder, biting her lip.

"Did I pass out?" I asked.

"I'm afraid you did, Old Spice," the cat said.

I propped myself up on my elbows. "I'm sorry, have we met?"

He rested a paw on my shoulder. "Not until just a few minutes ago, when you passed out in my library. I'm Jay Z. Catsby."

My jaw dropped. The wealthy socialite Jay Z. Catsby was an orange domestic shorthair with dark brown fur around his eyes. His white-tipped ears stood at attention. His mouth seemed stuck in a permanent frown.

"Shouldn't we call an ambulance? He needs a doctor," Cordon said.

Catsby shook his head. "There's no time."

I glanced around the room, which was stocked to the rafters with drums of ketchup, mustard, and other condiments. I wasn't in a hospital—and I wasn't on a bed at all. I was on a kitchen table. A woman passed by with a freshly made chopped salad. As she exited through a swinging double door, a cartoonish-looking gentleman entered the room. I recognized him from the subway as the famous plastic surgeon, Dr. Zeckleburg. His face was beginning to droop at the edges, as if he was melting. Perhaps he was.

"I've brought a doctor down to take a look at you," Catsby said.

"Does he know anything about internal medicine?" I asked. "Someone cut my one of my kidneys out. I believe the wound is causing me some trouble."

"Have I messed around inside a man's abdomen before?" Dr. Zeckleburg asked in a thick Eastern European accent. "Not professionally, no. But there's a first time for everything."

Jesus. I was about to be operated on my Hans Gruber.

"Can't we just go to a hospital?" I asked.

"Hospitals aren't very intimate, Old Spice," Catsby said, patting me on the back. His touch sent shivers of pain through my body, and I screamed on the operating table.

"Why do you keep calling me Old Spice?"

"Because you smell awful," he explained.

Dr. Zeckleburg produced a pill from his pocket. "Lucky for you I always carry roofies," he said, slipping it in my mouth...

CHAPTER TEN

When I came to, I was resting in the middle of a large bed. It was so big, in fact, that I couldn't reach either side if I'd stretched my arms out, giving me the feeling that I was afloat on a sea. A sea of comfort. Once again, Catsby was sitting next to me, attending to me. For a cat that no one had ever seen before, he and I were getting pretty chummy.

"How you feeling, Old Spice?"

"I wish you'd quit calling me that," I said. It wasn't an offensive name or anything, but I associated the cologne with my father, who liked to splash it on his bag after shaving.

"What would you have me call you, then?"

"My name: Dick."

Catsby mulled this over for a moment, as if it were a matter of some weight. Finally, he said, "Afraid I can't do that. 'Dick' is a perfectly fine name and all, but I feel we're too close for first names, Old Spice."

The hubris of this creature!

"I thank you for saving my life and all," I said, "but I don't know how close we are. I mean, we've only just met."

"And yet we share a special bond. Can you feel it? I certainly do. After all, it's not every day that I'm able to save a neighbor's life donating my own liver."

I gulped. "I was missing a kidney, not a liver. Besides, you only have one liver. Without it, you'd die within hours."

Catsby cocked his head. "Is that so? Dr. Zeckleburg!"

The surgeon strolled into the room. His "Kiss the Cook!" apron was spattered with blood.

"Doctor, I believe we may need to put the patient back under. Apparently, he was missing a kidney, not a liver. In any case, I believe it's imperative that I get mine back."

Dr. Zeckleburg sighed. "You can't make an omelet without breaking a few eggs, right?" He pulled another round pill out of his pocket and set it on my tongue. "We'll have you fixed up in no time."

CHAPTER ELEVEN

The next time I opened my eyes, Catsby was doubled over in pain in the chair. I was back in his bed, reclining.

"The bed's big enough for both of us," I said, surprised that I still had any voice left after all of the screaming I'd been doing.

Catsby sat up with his back flush against the chair. "You're a guest in my home. And now Dr. Zeckleburg has stitched you back up. I've got my liver back, and you have two kidneys once again."

"Where'd the extra kidney come from?"

"For legal reasons, it's probably best that you don't ever learn the answer to that question."

"Fair enough," I said. "I don't know how to thank you. You've been too kind."

"Think nothing of it," he said, waving his hand. "You're just lucky that we're both the same blood type.

You lost a lot of blood on the operating table, and we had to give you a transfusion."

I winced. "Don't take this the wrong way—I appreciate the gesture and all—but is our blood compatible?"

"Why wouldn't it be?"

"Well, you're...you're a cat."

"Obviously," he said. "What of it?"

"I'm a human."

"I don't think that's ever been in question."

I shook my head. "I wasn't disputing either of these facts, merely asserting them. I'll get to my point. I'm not a doctor, but I don't believe humans and cats have compatible blood."

"I see. You'll never hear me do this again, but—for your sake—I'm going to break character."

He leaned close to me and whispered three words that would forever change my perception of reality: "Don't tell anyone else, but I'm not actually a cat."

Okay, that was more like ten words, but you get the drift. I no count good.

"You're not a cat? What are you, then? A dog?"

"Don't be gross. I'm not going to remove my fursuit, but trust me when I say I'm a person underneath this heavy attire. I'm a human being."

"The costume's so real," I said.

"It had better be, for what I paid for it."

I marveled at the detail, right down to the wet pink nose. "Wait," I said, remembering I was in the midst of a major medical emergency. "What's your blood type?"

"I'm clean, if that's what you're asking."

"I'm not talking about diseases. I'm type A. I can only receive transfusions from donors with type A and O."

"Pretty sure I'm B. However, I'm a type A personality. Does that count?"

I shook my head.

"This is not good, Old Spice. Not good at all. Don't worry, though...we'll get you to the hospital and have them pump it out of you, and fill you back up with some fresh stuff."

Cordon entered the room and looked at me. I probably looked like death, but she looked as good as ever. Standing vigil at my bedside hadn't taken much out of her.

"If you'll excuse me, Old Spice—I need to speak with Cordon in private for a minute," Catsby said, rising from his chair and escorting her out of the room. I tried waving to her, but couldn't muster the strength to raise my arm. With my immune system fighting against the transfusion, I was destined for the grave if they didn't get me to a hospital soon.

This wasn't how I saw my life ending. I thought for sure that I would die being crushed to death between a stripper's breasts, or some other manly thing. At least I would die at a party. That would look good on my tombstone: "Dick Narroway. He died like he lived...at a party." And then maybe a little penis drawing under that. If there was enough money, maybe add a drawing of a butt on the back of the grave marker.

Cordon returned alone and sat down on the bed

next to me. "You won't believe what I just heard. It's the most amazing thing!"

"There's an ambulance on the way?"

"Oh, I don't know about that—I'm sure Catsby's calling one right now—but he told me a fabulous secret. I can't wait to tell you! If you live, that is."

"Could you just, you know, tell me now? I mean, I could be dead soon anyway."

"Don't be so morbid, Dick," she said, slapping me on the chest.

I coughed up a big loogie of blood, farted, we both laughed, and, once again, I lost consciousness.

CHAPTER TWELVE

It took me weeks to fight off the infection resulting from Catsby's ill-fated blood donation. There were several times my doctors thought I should have died, and a few times they may have actually tried to kill me because of awful things I allegedly said. When I get feverish I've been known to turn into a bit of an anti-Semite. If that makes me a "bad person," then I guess I'm "guilty as charged." Much to the chagrin of the Anti-Defamation League, I survived. My new Gentile doctor finally discharged me after fourteen days.

The bad news was that I would be able to return to work.

The good news was that I got a bona fide doctor's note for missing work, which would cover me back to the day I left early with Tucker for his little hotel party.

Tucker hadn't visited me in the hospital. Then again, I hadn't told him anything about the incident. I didn't mention it on social media either. All it would do would worry my friends and family, and I wasn't in the misery business. You might say I was in publishing and that's practically the same thing, but I digress.

On the train ride home, I answered a call from an unknown number.

"How you feeling, Old Spice?"

"Catsby," I said, recognizing the purr in his voice. "I'm feeling much better. Thanks for taking care of my hospital bill."

"I...didn't take care of it," he said slowly.

"That must be why they chased after me," I said. "Good thing I had my strength back."

"I was going to offer to pay your bill," he said. "Since it's not an issue any longer, though, why don't I take you out to lunch?"

My stomach grumbled. I hadn't eaten anything but hospital food for fourteen days. "I'm on my way home now. Did you want to go out today?"

"Works for me," he said. "You might want to meet me at the Jersey Shore first. It appears there's been an incident of some sort at your house. In fact, that's the main reason I called."

An incident? That didn't sound good; that sounded bad. Very bad. You don't call good things "incidents." When you say that Johnny had an "incident" at school, that probably doesn't mean he scored a 780 on his SATs. More likely, Johnny was caught playing with himself in the girl's locker room.

"What happened? A break-in?"

"I'm looking out the window right now," Catsby said, "and there are several fire trucks battling a blaze. I don't know how much of your house is left—there's too much smoke to tell. You didn't leave a gas burner running on your stove or anything, did you?"

Oh no.

Judi Dench.

CHAPTER THIRTEEN

When I stepped off the train, I saw the thin trail of smoke rising in the distance. My house. Or rather, the house my parents were renting for me. As I walked the ten blocks from the station to the beach, the smoke grew darker, confirming my worst fears. A block away, I saw there was nothing left of the house to return to. Three fire trucks were parked out front, hosing down the ashes like gardeners watering the lawn.

"What happened here?" I asked one of the firemen.

"Some idiot was keeping a pet dragon," he said, his Jersey accent thicker than a prime rib. "They're not even legal in this state. The cops are going to string this guy up by his nards, whoever the stupid dumbledore is."

"I hope they cut his nards off," I said, trying to throw him off my path. "I hope they paint them pastel colors and display them in the town square at Easter."

This pleased the fireman, for he nodded.

"So, uh, what happened to the baby dragon?" I asked.

"The dragon's on the loose," he said, "but I didn't say it was a *baby* dragon."

"You didn't?"

He narrowed his eyes at me. "I said *pet* dragon."

"That's interesting. I guess I just assumed, y'know."

"You just assumed," he said. "Say, what's your name, anyway? You live around here?"

I felt sweat beading on my brow, either because I was nervous or because the ashes were still plenty warm. "My name is...Nick Carraway. And I live—"

"—with me," a voice behind said. I whipped around. Catsby was standing on a yellow Segway. "Come on, Nick. Lunch awaits."

I saluted the fireman and climbed onto the Segway with Catsby. "Thanks for saving me," I whispered. "I owe you one."

He waved me off. "Think nothing of it, Old Spice. Consider ourselves even now."

The Segway lurched forward, and I wrapped my arms and legs tight around Catsby's torso. The ride was long and awkward; my arms and legs quickly tired. If I let go, however, I'd splatter on the pavement.

An hour later, as we crossed the George Washington Bridge, I broke the silence. "We're heading back into Manhattan," I said.

"I wouldn't eat out in New Jersey if my life

depended on it," Catsby said. "It's all dog food as far as I'm concerned."

After a few moments of silence, he asked if I knew what had happened to my bungalow.

"Not a clue," I lied.

Catsby, detecting my subterfuge, nodded. "We're friends now. If you were in some kind of trouble, I'd want you to come to me for help. You can trust me."

Could I, though? While my groin was pressed up against his back—and his tail was flopping in my face—I couldn't say we were friends. Not yet. I still knew next to nothing about him. I knew he had money, and that he had expensive and exotic tastes (in parties, in food, and in transportation). I also knew that he was a grumpy cat. His perpetual frown made everything that came out of his mouth sound a little salty, like an old, world-weary sailor.

"What is it you do again?" I asked, hoping to learn more about him.

"You could say I'm a shot caller," he said. "A baller."

"You play basketball."

"Oh, not since grade school, I'm afraid. *You* try dribbling a basketball with these paws." He raised his arms for me to see. "I don't really play any sports. That doesn't mean I don't love to play...games."

The way he said "games" made me a chill run up my spine. What was he into? One possibility was that he was a gambler. It wasn't a stretch to imagine illegal, high-stakes poker games taking place in his basement. His money had to come from somewhere—unless he'd inherited it. As someone who came from a decent amount of money, though, I understood just how sensitive the rich are to questions about their revenue streams. If he wanted me to know, he would tell me when the time was right.

"I hear you're a Midwest boy," he said. "I'm a Midwest boy myself."

"Yeah. I was born and raised in Chicago."

"The city proper or the suburbs?"

"Naperville," I said.

"Where'd you go to school?"

"Iowa."

"I've never been to Iowa," he said. "What's it like?"

"There are cornfields bigger than Walmart parking lots," I said. "Where'd you go to school?"

"Arizona."

"A credible institution."

"I suppose. After college, though, I didn't know what to do with my life. I decided to go into the military. They turned me down. Apparently cats can't serve in this country. Can you believe that? This is the twenty-first century. I'm sorry, I don't mean to bore you with all of this."

"No, no. Go on."

"Well, Old Spice, after that I did the only thing a cat can do. I lounged around in the sun during the day, and lounged around under the moon at night. A lot of lounging around."

A siren drowned out our conversation. Catsby glanced over his shoulder to see an NYPD cruiser, lights flashing, trailing us. He pulled the Segway over to the side of the road—we were in lower Manhattan now—and the car stopped behind us.

"License and registration, please," the female officer said.

Catsby pulled his wallet out of his suit jacket and pawed through it. "This Segway is unregistered, and I don't have a driver's license," he said, "but I do have this."

He handed a card over to the officer. She looked it over.

"My apologies," she said, passing it back. "Have a good day, gentlemen."

We continued on our way. "What was that all about?" I asked.

Catsby showed me the card. It was a Rite-Aid Wellness Rewards card. "I get one point for each dollar I spend there, and up to twenty-five points on every prescription. Once you reach a certain level—you'll know you've hit it, because they'll issue you one of these special platinum cards—you can use it to get out of traffic tickets."

The standard Walgreens Balance Rewards card on my keychain suddenly felt inadequate, like I was less of a man. I thought my family did well for themselves, but Catsby was clearly on a whole new level. The only question was, Why did he seem so grumpy all of the time? Was it just the permanent scowl on his furry headpiece, or did the sadness go deeper?

CHAPTER FOURTEEN

We stopped for lunch at the Times Square Applebee's. A valet tried to steer Catsby's Segway, but was immediately thrown off. The poor kid sailed over our heads and landed in the street, where he was backed over by a garbage truck. He pulled himself up off the ground.

"Don't worry, Mr. Catsby, we'll park your vehicle," he said, just before being struck by a taxi.

"Should we help him?" I asked, disturbed that no one was rushing to his aid. This time he wasn't getting back up.

"He'll be fine," Catsby said, "The Segway is a sentient model, and has grown attached to me. They'll get it under control. Eventually."

Catsby ushered me into the restaurant. I glanced over my shoulder at the valet. He was lying motionless in the street as car after car rolled over his lifeless body.

"Table for three," Catsby told the hostess.

"Are we meeting someone?" I asked.

"We are. I hope that's alright, Old Spice."

"Of course," I said. "I'm no stranger to threesomes."

The hostess grabbed a couple of menus and led us to a dark booth in the back of the restaurant, where a folf cosplayer was seated. The fursuited hugged Catsby, then extended a paw to me.

"Dick Narroway, I'd like you to meet an old friend of mine—Stratton Bellyflop."

"Pleased to meet you," I said, although I was anything but. Bellyflop was the notorious Folf of Wall Street. He'd risen to fame through a series of illegal stock schemes. He was also an out-and-proud folf (a fox and wolf hybrid). Despite the smile permanently plastered on his mask, he made me uneasy. Neither foxes nor wolves are domesticated dogs. They can snap at any moment and bite your hand off—just like stockbrokers.

"I see my reputation precedes me," he said, reading the look of abject terror on my face. There was a wicked glint in his eye, like he wanted to eat me. When Catsby had asked me to lunch, I hadn't counted on being the one eaten.

"I must confess to seeing your movie," I said, slipping into the booth next to Catsby. This put the table between the monster and me.

"That Scorsese flick? Half-truths and lies," he said, waving a paw dismissively. "I never used a straw to blow coke into a girl's butt. I mean, seriously, who does that? What if she farts? Then you've got coke all over the place. *That's* drug abuse."

A thin waiter with an even thinner mustache stopped at our table. "Y'all ready to order, or should I give you a minute?"

"Do you know what you want?" Catsby asked me.

I hadn't had a chance to look over the menu. "You guys order first."

"A round of Red Bull and vodkas for the table," Bellyflop said. "And what's your soup of the day?"

"It's just grease from the vat of fries."

"I'll take a cup of that, and a house salad."

Catsby ordered a bowl of Purina® Friskies® Grillers Meaty Tenders + Crunchy Bites™.

The waiter looked at me. "And you?"

"Oh," I said, stalling for more time. "What's good here? What do you recommend?"

The waiter shrugged. "I recommend you eat someplace else."

"He just got out of the hospital," Catsby said, snatching the menu away from me. "I'm sure your food can't be any worse than what he's had there. Just bring him one of everything."

"You got it," the waiter said, collecting the menus and rushing away.

"I'm hungry, but not *that* hungry," I told Catsby.

"Don't worry about it. It's my treat. We'll just take whatever you don't eat home."

I remembered I didn't have a home, but would worry about that later.

Bellyflop eyed me with his giant folf eyes. "So Catsby tells me you're looking for a business opportunity."

"An opportunity?"

"He says you're interested in becoming an independent business owner. An I.B.O."

Catsby cut in. "This isn't the guy I was telling you about. Dick's my neighbor."

"My apologies," Bellyflop said. "If you'll both excuse me, I need to freshen up in the men's room. Don't worry, I'm not going to do cocaine—unless either of you have any?"

We shook our heads.

Once he was gone, Catsby turned to me. "Did you watch the 2014 Super Bowl?"

"A terrible game," I said. "The Seahawks blew out Denver by like thirty-five points."

"Correct. Peyton Manning, one of the greatest quarterbacks of all time, put up eight points in one of the most important games of his career," Catsby explained. "That doesn't happen. I have it on good authority that the Broncos threw the game."

"Impossible," I said.

"It's true—the man that paid them off just left this table."

"The waiter?"

"Stratton. The Folf of Wall Street."

"Oh, that makes much more sense," I said. "He mentioned a business opportunity, though. After a windfall like the Super Bowl, doesn't he have enough money?"

Catsby shrugged. "Does one ever have enough? Plus, it's never been about the money for him. After you make your first billion, it's just paper. Stratton is addicted to the hustle. He can't stop playing the game."

Our waiter returned with a tray of Red Bull and vodkas. I wasn't in the habit of drinking before the sun went down, but you know what they say: When in Rome, drink up because you'll probably be buggered soon.

"Look here, Old Spice," Catsby said, sipping his drink. "I'm afraid I wasn't quite honest with you earlier. I had an ulterior motive for bringing you out to lunch today. Don't worry—it has nothing to do with Stratton. It has to do with Miss Bleu." Catsby didn't smile as he said this, but then he never smiled. He paused, clearly in no hurry to elaborate. I was beginning to feel played, like I was a mouse in Catsby's little game of cat and mouse. That would make him the cat.

"What is it?" I asked impatiently. "Let's hear it. I'm not big on mysteries."

"Really? If you've never read an Agatha Christie mystery, you're missing out on some great fiction."

"Mystery books I can handle. Real-life mysteries drive me nuts."

"There's no mystery here," he said. "I've just got a small favor to ask of you. Miss Bleu will elaborate. She should be stopping by any moment now. I—"

His phone rang, and he pulled it out of his jacket.

"This is Catsby... You what? Who's in charge.... Napier? Hold on." He covered the phone with a paw. "If you'll excuse me, Old Spice, I have to take this call."

Bellyflop returned just as Catsby was leaving.

"Always up to something, that cat," Bellyflop said, watching Catsby head for the door. "What a fine feline, wouldn't you say? A good-looking cat."

"Yes."

"He's an Arizona man."

"So I've heard."

Bellyflop nodded and smiled.

"Have you known him for a long time?" I asked.

"Many years. I had the pleasure of meeting him for the first time in a fantasy football league."

"Catsby never mentioned he played fantasy football."

"He was good at it—one of the best I've ever seen. Do you play any fantasy sports?"

I sipped my drink. "A little Magic the Gathering in my younger years, if that counts."

"You're a funny man," he said, without any hint of amusement.

Catsby returned. "Sorry about that. Business before pleasure."

"I apologize I can't stay for the pleasure," Bellyflop said, "but I must be off. Papa John awaits."

"You're skipping out of here to get pizza?" I asked.

He laughed. "I'm meeting Papa John, founder of the pizza chain. We are...business associates." I waited for him to elaborate, but he said no more on the subject.

I watched him leave, then I turned to Catsby. "Where do you suppose our food is?"

"They're cooking the entire menu for us," he said. "I'm assuming that will take a while."

I sighed. My eyes wandered around the room and stopped on a familiar face. Tucker Boobcannon. "Come along with me, I need to introduce you to."

Catsby raised his eyes in intrigue, but followed me to Tucker's table without asking any questions. Tucker was dining solo. He looked at me with confusion at first, but then a warm smile broadened on his face.

"Dick! I haven't heard from you since our little night out. I was beginning to worry about you. You looked pretty pale when we left you in the bathtub. I called around to morgues Monday morning just to be safe."

"It was nothing a two-week stay in an intensive-care unit couldn't fix," I said. "Anyway, I thought I'd introduce you to my neighbor. This is Mr. Catsby."

"Tucker Boobcannon," he said, making no effort to rise from his seat or shake hands with Catsby. "How do you do?"

"Not your wife," Catsby said quickly.

"Excuse me?"

"You asked who I did."

"I asked *how* you did," Tucker said.

"My apologies," Catsby said. "In that case, I'm doing very well, thank you."

Tucker turned back to me with a roll of his eyes. "Miley keeps asking about you. I told her you're a big boy, who can handle yourself. You're not like one of those nerds who needs someone to mommy them."

"Women worry," I said. "It's sweet."

I turned toward Catsby, but he was no longer there. He'd headed back to our table.

"What's with your friend?" Tucker asked. "Is he slow or something?"

"On the contrary," I said, "he's one of the sharpest cats I know."

"He was frowning like someone peed in his Cheerios. I tell you, the smarter someone is, the more likely they are to experience depression and anxiety. Fact. There's something to be said for being ignorant. It's the main reason I don't read. I can't risk exercising my brain. If I ever got smart, I'd end up all depressed like one of you eggheads." He paused. "No offense, Dick."

"None taken," I said. His argument was sound. In my experience, stupid people go through life with smiles plastered on their dumb faces, oblivious to all of the pain and suffering going on around them. Many of my friends in college had gotten elective lobotomies for this very reason. They couldn't wipe themselves afterward, but at least they weren't worried about the Middle East or the plight of baby carrots.

"Earth to Dick," a faraway voice said. Tucker snapped his fingers at me.

"Sorry," I said, returning to our conversation.

"I sometimes wonder what goes on in that head of yours. It's like you're writing a damn book in there."

"Maybe I'll write everything down someday, when

I'm old and nostalgic for the bygone days of yore. It feels like we're living in the best of times, and the worst of times. I look around and see the age of wisdom, the age of foolishness. It's the epoch of belief, the epoch of incredulity. It's the season of light, the season of darkness, the spring of hope, the winter of despair. We have everything before us and nothing before us. We—"

"We're all getting bored," Tucker said. "If you write a novel, don't include any of that garbage. Nobody has patience these days. Get right to the action."

"My life isn't exactly action-packed."

"Then don't write about your life. Write about someone else's. Like your furry friend. There's got to be a good story behind that scowl on his face."

It wasn't the worst idea in the world. If I wanted to capture the essence of the era, the zeitgeist of post-Great Recession America, why not write about the richest of the rich? The wealthy are living embodiments of the American dream. Everyone is fascinated by them. Nobody wants to read about poor people. Working in publishing, I knew just how true this was. Half the romances we published featured billionaire heroes; the other half featured zillionaire heroes. If I were to write about Catsby, though, the challenge would be to humanize him. I had to find out who the real Jay Z. Catsby was.

CHAPTER FIFTEEN

Later that afternoon, Cordon joined us at Applebee's. By that point, I'd eaten my way through about a quarter of the menu. I couldn't stop stuffing my face. When Catsby took my silverware away, I thrust two hands into my penne, shoveling pasta into my mouth like a toddler. Cordon averted her gaze, too embarrassed to watch. But let me tell you: I had no shame. No shame at all. After two weeks in the hospital, my appetite had returned in full force and then some.

"I think that's enough, Old Spice," Catsby said, pushing my plate into the center of the table. "If you eat any more, we're going to have to wheel you out on a stretcher."

I leaned back in the booth with a heavy sigh. As if on cue, the button on my jeans popped off and hit a passing waitress in the face. A thin mist of blood sprayed into the air as her head snapped up and to the left (a little Zapruder film that still plays in my head from time to time). Two cooks emerged from the back. They picked up the waitress's lifeless body and hauled her into the kitchen.

"I think I'm done," I said.

Catsby glanced out his phone. "Look at the time—I must be off. If you kids will excuse me...."

"Can I catch a ride back with you?" I asked.

"My business is in the city, I'm afraid." He handed me his Rite Aid card. "Take a cab home—on me, Old Spice."

I took the card from him. Such power, in the palm of my hand! The feeling quickly passed when I realized I didn't have a home to go back to. "My house—"

Catsby slapped a paw to his forehead. "I'm sorry, that's right. Why don't you stay with me until we can find you a new place?"

"I couldn't impose."

"It wouldn't be imposing. I have thirty-two rooms, only one of which I use. You'd practically have your run of the place."

"Thank you," I said, once again dumbfounded by his generosity.

After he left, I remarked to Cordon just how selfless Catsby seemed to me.

She smirked. "There's no such thing as a selfless cat."

"Then why help me? We're just neighbors—practically strangers, at that."

"You have something he wants."

I scoffed at her suggestion. "Impossible. He has all the money in the world. If there's something he wants, he could buy it in a heartbeat."

Cordon leaned over the table. "He can't buy your cousin."

"Miley? Tucker would probably sell her for the right price."

"What an awful thing to say, Dick. Women aren't property to be bought and sold."

"You're right," I said, readily conceding the point. Now was no time to get into my somewhat controversial views on prostitution.

"And besides, Catsby would never treat a woman that way—he's too classy."

"If you say so. What does he want with Miley, anyway? I've only heard her mention his name once, and that was when you brought it up at their place in Park Slope. Have they even met?"

"Oh, they've met," Cordon said. "Let's go for a walk through Times Square. I'll tell you everything I know."

CHAPTER SIXTEEN

As we strolled through the squalid crowds of human garbage in Times Square, Cordon related the entire sordid backstory of Catsby and Miley.

Although she was a Chicago girl now, Cordon was born and raised in Louisville, where she met my cousin on the regional beauty pageant scene. Cordon was a couple of years younger than Miley. Her pageant talent was hot dog eating, which she would one day turn into a lucrative career. Miley's talent was reading books. While a novelty on the pageant circuit, there was no money in it. My aunt and uncle decided to send her to college in Iowa, where she could at least put her talent to some use.

"The summer before Miley went to college, she was the talk of the town," Cordon told me. "We all thought she would become a model or something, and here she was talking about going to school to develop her brain!

It was such a foreign concept in Kentucky—a girl with looks *and* smarts.

"One morning, I was jogging past her house when she pulled up riding on the back of a moped. Her arms were around a young gentleman I'd never seen before. When they stopped in her driveway, she waved me over and introduced me to her friend. He removed his helmet, but not the brown paper bag underneath. His name was Shia Lebouf. We all know what eventually happened to him—"

—and here Cordon made the sign of the cross—

"—but at the time he was a rising Hollywood star. A major catch for a smalltown girl. He'd been in town at a film festival and met Miley in line at KFC. Five minutes later, they were making love in the bathroom. And five minutes after that was when I met them."

"Didn't you say this was in the morning? Does KFC serve breakfast?"

Cordon laughed. "This was Kentucky, darling—we eat at KFC three meals a day, and then some."

I shuddered with fear. Perhaps it was too soon to be discussing food, as I had forty-five pounds of Applebee's lodged in my bowels. I'd be backed up for days like traffic on the George Washington Bridge.

"Was it love?" I asked.

"I suppose. They started dating seriously after that. Shia even dropped out of the Transformers franchise to be with her."

I held out my hand. There was just something so romantic about transforming semi-trucks that put me in a semi-romantic mood. To my surprise, Cordon clasped hands with me. We continued our stroll, hand-in-hand, through the neon wasteland. Times Square was at once breathtaking and revolting, like a world-class BJ from an ugly hooker. Not that I would, uh, know anything about that.

"It's funny, but she's never mentioned Shia," I said. "I don't think Tucker's mentioned him either."

"Tucker doesn't know. It's better that way. You mustn't tell him."

"My lips are sealed," I said, clamping them tight together. "Mmmrwwmrmwmw."

"Can you open your lips again? I can't understand you."

"Sorry. I asked why they split up."

"They were walking downtown one day, and Miley stopped to watch some kittens in the window of a pet store. There was this one cat she just absolutely fell in love with. A cat the size of a human being.

"And this gigantic furball returned her gazing gaze! She swore to me they connected on some deep, mystical level. Now, Shia was no dummy. He could see it in her eyes. She would never love him as passionately as she loved that cat. He ran from her, tears streaming down his face, soaking the paper bag. It took Miley several minutes before she even noticed Shia was gone.

"Miley entered the pet store and approached the window display. The cat's cage had no lid—pet stores, like gun stores, encourage you to touch the merchandise. Miley stroked the kitten from forehead to tail, marveling outloud at his silken, luxurious fur. Never had she petted a cat so soft before!

"'My name is Miley. What's your name, little guy?'

"He craned his neck up at her, showing off his collar.

"She read his name aloud. Jay Z. Catsby."

I gasped at the revelation. "Gasp!"

"Catsby purred at the sound of his own name. There was a mysterious excitement in the air, the kind that usually happens at the height of summer when the days are long and anything is possible. Her heart beat quicker as Catsby brushed against her arm, rubbing his body on her as if to claim her as his own. He needed her just as she needed him.

"Miley approached an employee. 'How much is that kitty in the window?' she asked. 'The one with the waggling tail? I do hope that kitty's for sale.'

"The employee told her that, yes, the kitty was for sale. Catsby, decked out in the fursuit, had snuck into the pet store one night and crawled into the window display. They couldn't get him to leave. They'd thought about calling the cops, but customers seemed to be amused by the furry in the window. The pet store employee named a price, like twenty dollars or something.

"Of course Miley could afford it—her parents were well-to-do. For her sweet sixteen, they'd bought her a brand-new Maserati, a diamond necklace, and a labiaplasty. But money wasn't the issue. The problem was that she was going off to college. There's enough trouble on campus without adding pets to the mix. It could never work out. She thought for a moment that maybe she'd adopt Catsby and leave him with her parents—but, no. Catsby deserved to be with someone who loved him, not someone who would abandon him.

"Catsby watched her return his way. His eyes were full of hope and passion, and he no doubt expected Miley to liberate him right then and there.

"'Oh, if only I could make you understand,' Miley said, tears welling up in her eyes. 'What we have is special. I can already feel it. I wish we could just run away together, like Romeo and Juliet, only without the whole death part...but it would never work. My parents wouldn't help me out. They'd simply disown me if I didn't go to college. The question then becomes, how would we pay the bills? No offense, but you...you're a cat. And I'm just a dumb girl. I can read, but I still need to go to college and get my learn on. It just...it just wasn't mean to be. Goodbye, Catsby. Goodbye forever.' She ran off in tears."

I shot Cordon a look of disbelief. "Couldn't she have just, I don't know, asked him to remove his costume? They could have discussed things, like two rational people. I'm sure Catsby could have supported both of them. He's filthy rich now, at least."

"She's your cousin. Have you ever known her to be rational?"

"Point taken. Was that the last time they saw each other?"

"As far as I know. I didn't see Miley much after that,

as I began traveling more for hot-dog eating competitions—the circuit really heats up in late summer with all of the state fairs. Rumors circulated about Miley. Someone said her mother had caught her leaving the house with a suitcase in one hand and a bag of catfood in the other. I don't think she was all that serious. Where was she going to go without her parents' money? Was it just going to be her and Catsby, living out of a suitcase under bridges for the rest of their lives like a couple of tweakers? I never asked her about it, because it was none of my business. Miley didn't leave her house again until the day her parents drove her to Iowa. That was where she met Tucker, of course."

"Of course," I said. "They dated for four years, and were married just a few months ago back in Louisville."

"I didn't see you at the wedding."

"That's because I didn't go."

"Not a fan?" Cordon asked, batting her eyelashes at me coquettishly.

"I get too emotional at them," I said.

"I can't believe you cry at weddings. That's so sweet."

"Sorry. Did I say I got emotional? I meant drunk. I get drunk at weddings."

"Oh." She looked away, and I felt her fingers slipping from mine.

"But sometimes I get so drunk that I cry," I added, hoping to bring her back around to my side. It was too late, though. She let go of my hand. I could feel her shutting down. Oh well. You know what they say: Women—can't live with 'em, can't live with 'em.

"I heard the wedding was a big one," I said.

"It was," Cordon said, her voice wistful. "It was full of more pomp and circumstance than Louisville had ever seen. Hundreds of guests arrived from all corners of the country. They rented out the entire Seelbach Hotel, and the day before the wedding he gave her a bronzed bald eagle egg.

"I was one of her bridesmaids. Before we left for the rehearsal dinner, I found her sprawled out on her bed cradling the egg in one arm and a bottle of Seagrams in the other.

"'We're supposed to be at KFC in twenty minutes,' I told her.

"'Here,' she said, rolling the egg across the bed. 'Take this and give it back to that silly boy who wants to marry me. Tell him the show's over. Miley's not getting married tomorrow, no way.' Then she started bawling."

"Obviously she went through with the wedding," I said.

"Of course she did. Her mother chalked it up to cold feet, but I'm not so sure. I felt her feet, and they weren't cold. In fact, they were pretty warm."

"Did she say why she wanted to call the whole thing off?"

"No, but while her mother was slapping some good sense into her, I found something in her wastebasket.

Something that might have explained her odd behavior."

"A needle with heroin residue."

"Worse," she said. "A blue box from Tiffany's with a giant cat collar inside."

"I'm assuming you think this had something to do with Catsby."

Her eyes widened. "Who else?"

A pack of Elmos surrounded us, engulfing us in a sea of red fur. "I suppose you're right about it being from Catsby," I said, batting the street performers away. "It couldn't have been from Tucker—he's a dog man through and through."

"You can say that again," Cordon said.

"I suppose you're right about it being from Catsby. It couldn't have been from Tucker—he's a dog man through and through."

The Elmos continued tailing us. We ducked into a public restroom (also known as a "Starbucks"), where Cordon continued her story as we waited in line. "Miley and Tucker were married, of course, and that was it. They had all those kids. I assumed that she'd buried whatever feelings she had for Catsby...until a few weeks ago, when I asked you if you'd been to one of his parties. There was a big to-do in the paper when he bought his place on the Jersey Shore. I thought she'd read or heard about it, but evidently not.

"Let me ask you something: Don't you think it's a strange coincidence that Catsby bought that house so close to Miley, just after she moved to the city?"

I contemplated this. "Well, there are ninety million people in the New York City and New Jersey metro region."

"So you think it's a coincidence?"

"No, I'm just saying he could have bought a residence on the Jersey Shore because of its proximity to Manhattan—not to Miley. It sounds like he's well connected in this town. He probably has business here."

"So just a coincidence."

I shrugged. "Only Catsby knows. I'm just saying it's possible. Anyway, why does it matter? We're talking about a guy who used to sleep in a pet store window. Men do foolish things all the time."

"They certainly do," Cordon said. After a pause, she added, "There's one more foolish thing I'm supposed to relate to you. Catsby wants to know if you'll invite Miley out to the Shore some afternoon. Then he'll show up as if by accident. Since you're staying with him now, I guess it doesn't even have to be an accident."

"Why doesn't he invite her over himself? Why involve me?"

"You're her cousin. She trusts you. Tucker trusts you. No way would he let his wife go out to New Jersey by herself."

"I don't see why Tucker should care—he does whatever he likes. His wife should be allowed to do the same."

"You know men and their double standards," she

said.

I did. I knew them well. "So him moving to town, all of these parties...you think it was all for her. Sounds like a lot of work just for a girl."

"Like you said, men are fools."

"I didn't say we were fools. I said we were foolish."

She smiled wanly at me and took my hand again. "There's a difference?"

I drew her toward me, closer this time, and bent down until our lips touched. She greeted me hungrily. She used her tongue to trace the contours of my mouth, lapping at my face like a thirsty dog. She pushed me down onto the counter, spilling some poor schmuck's grande iced frappacino, the shouts and cries of the baristas fading into the background as we made love in the milky froth.

CHAPTER SEVENTEEN

When I returned to the Jersey Shore, I was afraid whatever was left of my house was on fire again. Nine o'clock in the evening and the whole shore appeared to be ablaze. As my cab turned the corner, I saw that the glow was coming from Catsby's house. Dozens of tents were pitched on his lawn, with lights of every color strung between them. There were rickety Ferris wheels and tilt-a-whirls as well, with carnies taking tickets and smoking. Mostly smoking, as there didn't appear to be anyone in attendance at this impromptu festival. Catsby strolled across the lawn to greet me.

"Your place looks like a county fair," I said.

"It does?" He surveyed his front yard unenthusiastically. "I guess so."

"Why else would you set up all these rides?"

He kicked the dirt. "I thought a carnival might be fun, that it might remind me a little bit of the fairs of my youth. But now I'm not so sure. It was a stupid idea. Let's get out of here, Old Spice. We'll take my Segway into the city."

"How about a raincheck? It's been a long day."

"It has been a long day, hasn't it? How did you and Miss Bleu get along?"

"We had...fun together. She's a tough one to read. One minute she's a good girl, the next she'll let loose the filthiest thing you ever did hear. We're going to a Yankees game on Saturday."

Here I paused, and Catsby waited for me to continue.

"She also mentioned that you and my cousin once knew each other," I said. "I'm going to text Miley and invite her over for lunch this week."

"Oh, that's not necessary. You don't have to go to all that trouble."

"It's no trouble at all. Really—I think she'd have a grand time. What day would work best for you?"

Catsby glanced around at the fair in progress on his lawn. "I'd probably want to have all of this cleared out first. How about later in the week, say, Thursday? Around noon."

I nodded. The chances of Miley being free during the day were close to a hundred percent. She didn't work, and had no children to care for during the day. Her days were like her nights, in that regard. The only problem was—

"I totally forgot that I have to work this Thursday," I said. "I've been off so long, I don't even remember what it's like. Maybe I could invite her over for dinner instead?"

"Dinner's too formal," Catsby said. "Say.... What if you didn't have to go back to work? What if you came to work for me, Old Spice?"

If you've been following my story so far, you know that my job was about more than money. On the other hand, I was already disillusioned with the publishing industry. Scrubbing the serial numbers off fanfiction had run me down long before I landed in the hospital.

"What do you propose?" I asked. "This doesn't have anything to do with your folf friend, does it?"

"Oh, no, nothing to do with him," Catsby said, shaking his head. "It is...confidential, though. I'd need to know if you're interested, before I tell you. It's just this little business I run on the side."

"You're not a bootlegger, are you?"

"Oh, heavens no. Moonshine is so Boring Twenties. Have you ever heard of a business called Amway?"

"Isn't that a pyramid scheme?"

He recoiled at my question. "'Scheme' is a strong word. Amway is a business that levels multi-level marketing techniques to maximize sales and growth for entrepreneurs. We sell consumer goods like healthcare products and jewelry."

"But the more people that sign up to sell Amway underneath you, the more you make, right? Isn't that a pyramid?"

"It's more like a triangle."

"Aren't pyramids and triangles the same thing?"

Catsby sighed. "Let's agree to disagree. Bottom line is, thanks to Amway, I have money. Now, being rich isn't as thrilling as I'd assumed it would be. I always thought when I had money that I'd *have money*. Like Scrooge McDuck. Have you ever seen *Duck Tales*? That guy had a roomful of coins that he swam in."

"It sounds unsanitary. Every year or two there's a study that examines what's on our currency, and fecal matter tops the list. Well, fecal matter and cocaine."

"Sounds like the makings of a great party," he said. "In any case, I've been looking someone to manage my money. Since you work with books, you seem like the logical choice."

"We might be talking about two different types of books," I said. "I'll take a look, though, if it will make you feel better."

"It would, Old Spice. It would. But let's worry about all that later. As you said, it's late. I'll show you to the room I've set up for you, and you can get some sleep."

He led me through his house, which I only vaguely recognized without the throngs of partygoers. The place looked badly in need of remodeling—a woman's touch, specifically. Not surprising, since Catsby was also in need of a woman's touch. Perhaps Miley could turn his frown upside down. Putting them back in touch was risky, though, as Tucker would certainly not approve. But isn't everybody owed some sort of happiness in this world? Even if only for a few hours, over tea. I called Miley from my room once I settled in for the evening. It was after midnight, but I knew she and Tucker kept late hours.

She answered on the second ring. "I thought you were dead!"

"The rumors of my death were greatly exaggerated," I said, stealing a quote from Mark Twain. He wasn't using the phrase any longer—he was dead now, no exaggeration.

"Don't joke about death. You always say such morbid things. Sad to say, I think I'm coming around to see it your way."

"You're becoming a misogynist?"

"A massage therapist, Dick? I could use a good deep-tissue massage after the week I've had. The kids are hell. Hell, I say! At least that's what the nanny says."

"Then why don't you take a day off from the Park Slope rat race. Come out to the Shore for lunch some day. Like Thursday."

"Aren't you working?"

"I've got a new gig. I'll tell you all about it over tea. Just you and me. No one else, especially not anyone you used to know or anything."

"Make it a Long Island iced tea and I'm in."

"It's a deal," I said. After I hung up, I began trying to formulate a plan to get an iced tea all the way from Long Island to New Jersey without the ice melting.

CHAPTER EIGHTEEN

I spent the week shuffling through boxes of financial records in Catsby's office while Catsby supervised the teardown of the fair. I couldn't make heads or tails of all the numbers, which were little more than illegible scrawls on napkins. Catsby needed a real financial advisor, not an ex-publishing intern. If anyone in publishing knew dick about finances, they wouldn't be working in publishing. But Catsby reassured me there was no one he'd rather have working for him, because he could trust me. He was big on trust. But did I trust him?

Thursday arrived with a thunderous boom. It was pouring rain, which meant we wouldn't be having Long Island iced teas on his back porch overlooking the sea. Local businesses hated rainy summer days, because they killed tourism. However, a good rain every once in a while cleaned the sidewalks of all the tanning lotion and vomit.

Around eleven, I realized I hadn't seen Catsby all morning. I searched the house for the proprietor to no avail. He'd just up and disappeared.

"Have you seen your boss?" I asked the butler, who I caught playing Wii in the main living room. One of the main living rooms, at least.

"You're not likely to, on a day like this. Master Catsby is deathly afraid of thunderstorms."

"For what reason?"

He looked at me cockeyed. "Why, he's a cat of course."

"Of course," I said deliberately. Sure, I'd gotten a few glimpses into his distinctly feline behavior, such as eating cat food. But cat food is delicious. (At least the wet stuff. I've never had any of that dry crap.) Being spooked by thunderstorms put Catsby on a whole other level. Was he so far "in character" that he'd forgotten Miley was visiting today?

"You look worried," the butler said. "I can assure you Master Catsby will be fine."

"I just hope this storm passes soon. My cousin's coming over for lunch, and I think he'd be interested in meeting her."

"Of course. He told me all about it. I'm having the kitchen prepare lunch as we speak. P.B. and J sandwiches with the crust cut off, and Long Island iced tea."

Before I could thank him, the front door swung open with blusterous force. We raced down the stairs and found Catsby standing in the doorway. His standard three-piece suit was dripping wet, soaked like a plush chair at a Josh Groban concert.

"I thought I'd go for a walk," he said glumly.

"Miley should be here within the hour," I said. "We need to get you toweled off. She's not going to be too impressed by you if you're looking like a wet dog."

The butler rushed off to find a towel. "Who says she's going to be impressed by me anyway?" Catsby complained. "It was a stupid idea. I doubt she'll want to see me."

"Don't say that."

"Has she ever mentioned me, Old Spice? Be honest, now."

"I can't say that she has," I said. "But that doesn't mean she doesn't still care about you. Stop being such a pussy."

"But that's what I am—a pussy cat."

"You're so much more, and you know it. Going out into a storm like this was a brave thing to do."

"I thought I'd get hit by lightning. I wouldn't be such a nervous wreck if I were dead."

"You aren't getting off that easy. If what they say is true, you have nine lives."

"That's just an old wives' tale. Cats are like everyone else in this world: We have one life to life."

"Let's get you out of your clothes. And take that wet fursuit off—"

"The fursuit stays on," he snapped.

"Sorry. I didn't mean anything by it."

The doorbell rang. His panicked eyes met mine, and in them I saw the depths of his fear.

"Go dry off," I said. "I'll take Miley to the dining room and stall for time. You can do this, Catsby. I believe in you."

Catsby crawled up the stairs on all fours. The sight of him running around like an ordinary house cat worried me. He seemed to be falling apart. If he'd truly bought his mansion here just to be close to Miley, then how sad it would be to be so close to the goal line and fumble.

I took a deep breath and opened the door. Miley stood on the porch, umbrella in hand. She looked as dazzling as ever. I had half a mind to ask her out myself.

"Are you going to let me in, Dick?"

"Sorry," I muttered, ushering her inside. I stowed her umbrella in a solid-gold umbrella stand. It had probably cost Catsby more than most men made in their lifetimes.

"So this is your place?"

"A friend's, actually. I'm just staying here temporarily."

"Friends are so wonderful, aren't they? If you don't mind me asking, what's your friend's name?"

"His name? His name...is Catsby."

There was a long pause as she tried to suppress her shock. Before she could compose herself, Catsby emerged into the entryway. He'd thrown a clean suit on over his fursuit. He still looked haggardly, but was at least walking on two legs again. He stopped at the bottom of the staircase. For several minutes, nobody said anything. You could feel the awkwardness in the air, like when your mother catches you tugging one out under the covers.

Miley let loose a little laugh. "I'm awfully certain to see you glad again."

"Excuse me?" Catsby asked, confused.

"I mean, I'm glad to see you're certainly awful."

The words were there, but not in the right order.

"You know what I mean," she said finally.

Catsby shrugged. "I guess."

"It's been forever since I've seen you."

"Nearly four years to the day," he said. "And you look as beautiful as ever."

At this, Miley blushed. "You're such a liar."

"There are two things you should know about me," he said, slinking toward her. Catsby seemed to have suddenly regained some of his lost confidence. "I like big butts...and I cannot lie."

Miley blushed. She had some curves on her, that girl.

"I'll just let you two catch up," I said, backing out of the room. They didn't appear to notice me leaving, even after I purposefully knocked over a flower vase and half-heartedly kicked the spilled dirt around for a few minutes. I sulked away, my heart heavy with the distinct feeling like I'd just become a secondary character in my own narrative.

CHAPTER NINETEEN

After an hour in one of Catsby's many bathrooms playing Angry Birds on my phone, I returned to the foyer. Catsby and Miley had taken their reunion elsewhere. I checked the dining room. Also empty. That's when I heard laughter from one of the living rooms. I peaked into the room and found Miley and Catsby on separate ends of the couch. I'd been worried their reunion would be painful for one or both of them, and I'd have to mediate. They didn't look up when I walked in. Neither of them was crying. A good sign.

"Ahem," I said, making an obnoxious attempt to clear my throat.

Catsby whipped his head around. "Oh, hello, Old Spice."

I motioned to the picture window, where a steady stream of sunshine was making its way in. "It's finally stopped raining. Just thought I'd let you know."

"You're a regular ol' weatherman, aren't you, Dick?" Miley said.

"Indeed he is," Catsby said jovially. His spirits seemed greatly improved. I'd never seen such a change in someone before. Although the frown was still on his face—it was a permanent feature of his fursuit, after all—he was positively radiant with good vibes. Miley was all smiles as well. If they could have a little bit of happiness, even for an afternoon, who was I to be a cockblock?

"I should leave," I said.

"No—stay," Catsby said. "Now that the storm has passed, we'll all go out on my boat this afternoon."

"You have a boat?" Miley asked, eyes wide.

"A yacht," he said. "It's parked out back. We can go ram some icebergs."

"I hadn't planned on dying today," she said.

Catsby shrugged, as if he had prepared for this eventuality. "Then we can just drive it down the coast, anchor it in front of Chris Christie's beach house, and knock some golfballs through his windows."

We all agreed this sounded like a lovely way to spend the rest of the day. After lunch—Miley downed so many Long Island ice teas it was a miracle she could still stand—Catsby dragged me back to his master bedroom to find me something appropriate to wear. I was still in my open-backed hospital gown. Catsby was tired of looking at my ass every time I turned around.

Catsby disappeared into his walk-in closet, and

returned twenty minutes later with a stack of polo shirts of every conceivable color under the sun (and a few colors only possible in other solar systems). He chucked them at me, one after another in rapid succession. I dodged the first two, but the third one caught me square in the face. The fourth hit me in the stomach, knocking the wind out of me. The fifth took me off my feet. I fell onto the bed, where Catsby continued to pile shirts on top of me.

"I can't breathe!" I said, attempting to claw my way out of the pile.

Catsby extended a paw to me and pulled me to safety. "I was just trying to have a little fun with you, Old Spice. Sometimes I get a little carried away, is all."

"Not all of us have your catlike reflexes."

"I'll try not to let it happen again."

I held up a blue polo shirt. It looked about the right size. A large painting above his cat bed caught my eye, however. "Is that who I think it is?"

He glanced up at the painting, which featured a regal-looking gentleman in a maroon jumpsuit. "Sir Catrick Stewart," he said.

"Are you a Star Trek fan?"

"Not particularly," he said with a sneer. "I'm a Catrick Stewart fan. He's one of the most prominent furries of our time. The first non-fleshie Star Trek caption. He's done a lot of good for the community. I wouldn't be where I am today without the paths he trailblazed."

"I saw him the other week, in Park Slope. He lives near Miley."

"You don't say?"

"I do say. I mean, I just said."

"It's a small world, isn't it? Everyone knows everyone. It's almost as if there's a writer in a room somewhere, working with a limited cast of characters. Not a very good writer, based on the sheer number of coincidences."

"It's in our nature to see connections between people and events," I said. "I don't think novelists should have to apologize for that."

"You sound like a writer."

"I have all these ideas for books, but never any time to write them," I lamented. I did a lot of lamenting back in the day.

"I saw how many drinks you were able to toss back at lunch today. You've definitely got the writer's temperament," he said. "And you say you have all these ideas, but no time? Here's how you become a writer, Old Spice: Make a butt-load of money, and then hire a team of ghostwriters to develop your ideas into books. That's what I would do."

I slipped the polo shirt on over my hospital gown. Catsby saw money as the answer to every problem. However, there are some problems money can't solve. It was with Catsby that I first began to develop my own theories about life and wealth, and I could already see that our paths would shortly diverge. I'd come out East to escape my privilege, only to be confronted with more money and privilege than I'd ever seen before. Or something like that. Who knows just what I was thinking, since I was literally sweating alcohol.

Catsby looked me up and down. "It looks like we still need to get you some pants."

He went back into his closet and returned, moments later, with a stack of sweatpants—which he proceeded to rifle at me, just like he'd done with the shirts. By the time I was finally dressed head to toe, there were so many clothes on the floor that it looked like an I.E.D. went off inside an American Apparel. I started picking the clothes up, but Catsby told me not to bother. "My butler will be by to sweep them up and burn them in the incinerator."

As Catsby and I boarded his enormous yacht—which, oddly, I'd never noticed docked just off the beach—I caught him pawing at the horizon. I'd seen him do this once before, the first night I'd laid eyes on him.

"What's out there?" I asked, peering across the ocean. Miley, who was already feeling queasy from imbibing over lunch, disappeared into the main cabin to "get her sea legs." I think that meant she was going to throw up.

"Miley's out there—or she was," Catsby said, gazing into the distance. "On clear evenings, there's this red light that dances around in the direction of New York City. I used to imagine it was Miley signaling me. Of course I knew it was nothing—a boat, I guess. But I liked to think she was out there, letting me know to not give up on us. That someday our paths would cross again."

There was a long silence.

"Wow," I said. "That's kind of messed up."

"I thought it was romantic."

I shook my head. "Do yourself a favor and don't ever tell Miley about this red light. She's here now. Just let it be what it is. A couple of old friends having a good time. Don't overthink it—and more importantly, don't let her know you've been thinking about her this much. Nothing turns a girl or guy off faster than a creeper."

"Huh. You bring up some interesting points, Old Spice."

Miley reappeared. "This boat is amazing! I can't believe you have an Olive Garden on here. Where did you ever get such a thing?"

"I won it in a poker game against a fellow named Earl Grey. The poor guy had a nasty gambling problem. His loss, my gain."

"You certainly have changed a lot since I saw you in that pet store window," Miley said. I swore I could detect a hint of sadness in her voice, as if she was nostalgic for the kitten she once knew—much in the same way Catsby was in still in love with that striking Kentucky girl he'd made eyes with all those years ago. Then again, I could have been overanalyzing the situation. Wasn't I the one who'd just told Catsby to stop overthinking things? Everything seemed to be coming together quite nicely. The good times couldn't last forever, but, hey, enough with the half-assed attempts at foreshadowing.

CHAPTER TWENTY

The day seemed to go on forever. Just when I was beginning to think Miley would leave her family and move in with Catsby—God knows there was enough room even if she brought her eleventy-thousand children—she returned home to New York.

That afternoon wasn't the last time I saw her around Chalet Catsby. Not by a long shot. As the summer wore on, she visited the Jersey Shore several times a week. How she did so without raising her husband's suspicions was beyond me, but I suppose he was tied up with his mistress. For my part, I kept my mouth shut about the whole thing. Other people's problems, yo.

Around the first of August, I was shooting clay pigeons in one of Catsby's living rooms when the doorbell rang. Catsby and Miley were aboard his boat, I think. They'd invited me—they always did—but I'd declined. In my experience, third wheels only work on tricycles. I waited a minute for the butler to answer the door, but he was obviously preoccupied. Whenever Catsby left the house, he seemed to disappear. When the cat's away...

I opened the door a crack. A timid-looking fellow wearing thick-rimmed glasses and a fedora was standing on the doorstep, rocking back and forth on his feet.

"Can I help you?" I asked, shotgun still in hand.

He gulped. "I'm, uh, looking for Mr. Catsby."

"He's not available," I said. "Can I take a message?"

"I'm a reporter with the *Daily Peanut,*" the man choked out. Ah. I'd known a few reporters back in my college days, but hadn't realized they were still around. The Great Recession had killed off most of the newspapers. These days, most of them just sat at home in their underwear banging out thousand-word recaps of episodic TV shows.

"What's this regarding?" I asked.

"Just wondering if he has, uh, anything to say, about—"

I slammed the door in his face before he could finish. Like I had time for his stammering act? I was stinking drunk at one in the afternoon, answering the door in my old hospital gown. You might say I'd been in a bit of a funk since breaking things off with Cordon. After that passionate day in Times Square, we hooked up a few more times, the last of which was around the middle of July. I know it was after Independence Day, because she'd already won the world-famous Statham's Hot-Dog Eating Competition on the fourth of July. After we bumped uglies that last time, our relationship fizzled out. It was a typical occurrence in those days: My phone died. I couldn't find the charging cable, so that was it. With no way to text Cordon, we just sort of drifted apart.

In the aftermath of our breakup, there was little reason to get out of bed. I had an entire library branch just down the hall from my room, but couldn't muster the energy to read. It was as if the life had been sucked out of me. Why had ever I left my life of relative comfort? I was tempted to return home to Naperville and crawl back up into my mother's womb. When I talked to her on the phone, however, I learned there was no room at the inn. She was pregnant. Probably my father's child, but who could tell with them anymore?

What about the job, you ask? The one Catsby'd offered me? Well. Ahem. Despite my debilitating depression, I was still technically employed as his financial consultant. He seemingly hadn't noticed that all I was doing was shifting papers from one filing cabinet to another. The numbers, as I've said, made no sense to me. My eyes blurred just looking at them. Or maybe the blurring was related to my alcoholism. Either way, I don't think Catsby even cared what I was or wasn't doing in his office on the rare occasions I showed up for "work." Even a casual perusal of his records through blurred eyes led me to believe his story about being an Amway salesman was grade-A horse manure...but, again, other people's problems.

When Catsby returned from his daily sojourn with Miley, I pulled him aside and mentioned the curious visit from the *Daily Peanut* reporter. After a brief look of concern on his face—a flash of nervousness I hadn't seen him exhibit since his reunion with Miley—he relaxed.

"Grab some wine coolers from the fridge and wait for me out back by the swimming pool. I'll send Miley on her way, and then it'll just be you and me, Old Spice. I think it's time I told you the truth."

Catsby was rumored to be involved in any number of schemes. I'd heard all of them: that he'd killed a man in Reno just to watch him cry, and then tried to kill Johnny Cash for taking credit for his life story. I could either sit here and go through every rumor one by one and debunk them, or I could tell you his story, from beginning to end.

Really? You want option number one?

Sorry. That's not how books work. At least the kind of books I grew up reading and writing, unless you count Choose Your Own Adventure books. No, the book you're reading right now has one course, charted by yours truly. Strap in and enjoy the ride. If you hate it, leave a nasty review on Goodreads or Amazon. See if I care.

So here it is: Catsby's story, as true as James Deen is long...

CHAPTER TWENTY-ONE

In his early twenties, Catsby had been a systems administrator for a health care company in Louisville. He went by a different name back then, of course—a name that he declined to tell me. One summer, on a lark, he went to a local comic book convention. He didn't read comic books, but that was beside the point; you couldn't find an actual comic book at a comic book convention if you tried. It was more of a pop culture convention.

There were, however, plenty of superheroes: fans in costume, parading through the aisles. Although Catsby was a straight male, his eyes didn't linger on the ample bosom spilling out of Wonder Woman's stars-and-stripes corset. Nor did he pay much attention to the female Thor, whose ass was harder than her hammer. Instead, he found himself staring at the cosplayers dressed as animals. They looked like college sports mascots, covered from head to toe in furry costumes.

They intrigued him. At first he was unsure of the reason. Upon reflection, he realized he'd always been drawn to anthropomorphism. He felt a kinship with animals that could walk and talk, from Tony the Tiger to Bugs Bunny. A quick unfiltered Google search later, and he discovered what he'd been all along: Catsby was a furry.

"I blew all my savings on a feline fursuit of my own," he said. "Not the one you see today, but a cheap one, a ragged old thing that had seen better days. I wouldn't be caught dead in it today, but at the time it served its purpose. Every night after work, I zipped it up and became a new man. Or, rather, a new cat."

He stayed in character longer and longer, to the point that it was emotionally painful to remove. The real "costume" was the suit he put on for work. He was no longer the guy who became a cat at night; he was a cat who became a guy during the day.

He saved his money to buy a new fursuit—one of the highest craftsmanship, created by a Florida costume designer recommended to him in a furry chat room. Once he put it on, he stared in the mirror. What he saw took his breath away. It couldn't have been more perfect. Even the frown sewn onto the suit's headpiece fit his grumpy disposition nicely. He'd always loved animals, but humanity? Humanity he'd loathed. He would permanently wear his contempt on his face. He quit his job, took the name "Jay Z. Catsby," and broke into the closest PetCo in order to live amongst his tribe.

The pet store employees discovered Catsby the next morning sleeping in the window display. Shockingly, they didn't call the police or kick him out. Maybe they figured he would be good for business. The other kittens in the window didn't seem to mind his presence either. In fact, Catsby claimed that after a few days, he even began to communicate with them through meowing. I wasn't sure if I believed him.

Turns out it was the most plausible part of his story.

The other cats—two boys and two girls, all from the same litter—had never met their birth parents. Most cats never meet their own fathers, and most are separated from their mothers at birth. That's just the cat's lot in life, Catsby said. You can't throw a feather toy without hitting a broken home.

Although the other cats accepted him as one of their own, their makeshift family didn't last long. After a week together, they began disappearing one by one from the window display. They weren't there to make friends; they were there to be adopted. After a store employee plucked Feline Dion out of the window display, Catsby turned to his last remaining sibling. "Looks like it's just you and me, brother."

Tomcat Petty yawned. "Brother? Listen, I like you, but we ain't brothers. And I don't know about you, but I can't wait to get out of here. If I have to spend one more night listening to those dogs whimper, I swear I'm going to claw my own throat."

"Except we're declawed."

Petty examined his paws, fear growing on his face.

"If you think that's bad," Catsby continued, "don't look between your back legs."

"What did they do— Oh, hell, no," Petty said, inspecting himself. "Hmmm. Maybe they're like your first pair is like baby teeth. They could grow back even bigger."

Catsby said nothing.

"Let's bust out of here," Petty said, pawing at the glass that surrounded them on all sides. PetCo wanted them to see the outside world, to see the menagerie of other animals on display, to make them feel their helplessness. Had their captors taken the dogs' claws as well? Did the parakeet have its testicles? Did birds even have testicles?

"Bust out of here? We have it pretty damn good in here," Catsby said. "Where would you go?"

"Home," Petty said.

Catsby scoffed at this. "You don't even know what that word means. As you said yourself, you have only the slightest recollection of the circumstances surrounding your birth. You don't know how good we have it in here."

Petty yawned and drifted to sleep. Just like that—right in the middle of the afternoon, right in the middle of their conversation. He'd forgotten about his little revolution. Catsby, however, couldn't shake the feeling that life was pointless. Inside. Outside. Wherever. He stood alert, one paw on the glass, tracking the movements of the people on the sidewalk. What if a family adopted him? Would he go home with them? He had a family of his own, a family that had disowned him after he came out as a furry. Perhaps a new family was in order. One that would accept him—

A pretty young girl placed her hand on the other side of the window, interrupting his thoughts. Although they could not touch through the glass, there was a connection there. Catsby's eyes met this girl's, and he suddenly saw that this relentlessly bleak life had but one true silver lining: love.

"I loved everything about her: her hair, her eyes, her lips," Catsby said. "Even her voice. Her voice was like—"

"Money," I said, nodding. "Her voice is like money."

He stared at me. "No, Old Spice. Her voice sounds like Peter Griffin."

"Does it?" I asked. The more I thought about it, the more I saw that he was right. My cousin sounded exactly like the *Family Guy*.

Of course, the romance between Miley and the grumpy cat in the window was fated to be short-lived. Cordon had already told me my cousin's side of the story, so there's no need to recount it here. Suffice to say, it was during that encounter that Catsby learned that love—that uplifting feeling that warmed his cockles—had its own anti-silver lining: heartbreak.

CHAPTER TWENTY-TWO

Heartbreak was only the beginning of Catsby's incredible tale. After Miley ran away in tears, he made up his mind. He would prove his worth to her. He would find a way to support them both, and—most importantly—do so without removing his fursuit.

The task wasn't as impossible as it seemed. Dozens of animals had made their own way in the world over the years. Some ran for political office, like Stubbs, a cat elected mayor of a small Alaskan town in 1997. Catsby wasn't very politically minded. No, he decided the likeliest route to success as an animal would be as an actor. While he may have passed for a cat in the window, he knew that he still had much to learn before he could pass as one on the big screen. There was one furry who'd made his way in the fleshie world without removing his fursuit, and he'd done it in Hollywood. Sir Catrick Stewart. Catsby would find him.

Before he could leave the pet store behind, a bearded and bespectacled gentleman approached him. "Hello, little kitty cat. My name is Doctor Schwing. What is your name?"

Catsby cocked his head and stared at the man.

"Oh, don't be shy," Dr. Schwing said. "I only wish to parley with you."

"I'm afraid I don't know the meaning of that word," Catsby said, embarrassed at his lack of culture. Petty continued napping.

"I mean, my good cat, I only wish to speak with you. Just a moment of your time."

Catsby shrugged. He had nothing else to do. Plus, this man was the first upright ape who'd understood his meows. "My name is Jay Z. Catsby."

Dr. Schwing clapped maniacally. "Excellent, excellent. What an amazing name for a kitten. Tell me, dear Catsby, were you born to a mother on the grounds of a factory farm? Do you remember a barn, perhaps?"

"My brother here might. What kind of doctor are you?"

"The only type that matters to you and your kind," Dr. Schwing said. "A veterinarian."

A chill ran down Catsby's spine.

"Don't worry, Mr. Catsby," the doctor said, sensing Catsby's alarm. "I'm not here to hurt you. I know your experiences with vets haven't been that pleasant, thus far. While I do not make apologies for those in my profession who hurt fair creatures such as yourself, you have my deepest sympathies."

"Easy to say, for a man who still has his balls," Catsby said.

"I cannot give you back what's been taken, but there are certain procedures that can be done. If you help me, then I can help you. You have my word."

Catsby sighed. What did he have to lose? Nothing. He'd already lost everything, including the love of his life. Perhaps this Dr. Schwing could help him get to Hollywood. "Tomcat here was born in a barn. I'm sure he'll be willing to help you. What do you want with us, anyhow?"

"I'm on a mission of vengeance. It's not a pleasant business, I'm afraid, but I think you'll see how necessary it is once you learn the particulars. The men who run the factory farm you were born on are real bad motorscooters. I'll need your brother's help to get past the front gates—I figure someone will recognize him, and let us in. Once we're in—"

A teenaged employee approached Dr. Schwing. "Hey, stop talking to him like that."

"Like what?" Dr. Schwing asked.

"Like that. Using them big words. Knock it off."

"Let's calm down, okay? I'm simply a customer, trying to conduct a transaction."

The boy's face reddened. He showed no signs of backing down. "We don't want your business. Whatever you're into, take it elsewhere. These cats aren't for sale."

"Let's not be ridiculous." Dr. Schwing pulled his

wallet out and began counting out hundred-dollar bills. "For everything, there is a price. Am I correct?"

"Don't make me get my manager," the kid said. His resolve was unwavering.

Dr. Schwing returned the bills to his wallet. "Get your manager."

The boy scowled at the doctor and sped off to the back of the store, brushing past a handful of customers oblivious to the mounting tension. Catsby looked at Dr. Schwing blankly, confused as to why this man would go to so much trouble to buy their freedom. Dr. Schwing smiled down at Catsby, a gentle smile that let him know that all his questions would be answered, in time.

The employee returned with a middle-aged woman. She had short hair and an even shorter fuse, and carried a cordless phone in her hand. "You'd better leave, mister, or we'll call the cops."

"I was simply trying to ascertain—"

She started dialing on the phone, but before she could even make it to the second number on the keypad, there was a loud crack like a firework had gone off inside the building. The phone lay on the ground in pieces; in Dr. Schwing's hand, smoke trailed from the tip of a handgun. The two employees were too shocked to move or speak, but customers ran out of the building in a mad dash.

"Let's go, Catsby," the doctor said, lifting Catsby into his arms. "Wow, you're...a...heavy one."

"Why don't I walk, and you carry Tomcat?"

Dr. Schwing picked up Tomcat Petty, who opened and closed his eyes as if to say, "Whatevs." The poor dumb animal had snored through the whole commotion, not even opening an eye after the gunshot.

Catsby finally had a purpose to his life.

He was somebody.

He was...CATSBY UNCHAINED.

CHAPTER TWENTY-THREE

"Wait a minute," I said. "This sounds exactly like the movie *Django Unchained.*"

"Never seen it," Catsby said.

"Are you sure? Instead of a dentist freeing a runaway slave, you're telling me about a vet freeing a couple of kittens from a pet store. I think you've even copied some of the dialogue, nearly word for word."

Catsby considered this. "Hmmmm. What an odd coincidence."

"I don't think it's a coincidence. It's called plagiarism."

"Let's split the difference and say it's an homage."

I stood up. "Either way, it doesn't sound like *your* story. It sounds like Quentin Tarantino's. You've opened your house to me. You've opened your financial records to me. Why can't you open your heart? Be honest with me."

"You're right, Old Spice. Sit back down. I'll pour us

a couple more margaritas and then I'll tell you the rest of the story—sticking closer to the facts."

"You don't need to dress up your story with shootouts and explosions to make it interesting," I said, sliding back into my chair. "Just tell me your story, in your own words."

"Of course. Let me ask you a question: Have you ever seen the movie *We're the Millers?*"

I shook my head.

Catsby nodded. "Then let's start the story over. I'll begin with the family that adopted me from that pet store: the Millers…."

CHAPTER TWENTY-FOUR

Six false starts later, Catsby finally relented to stop telling stories and start telling the truth. He hadn't been freed by a gun-wielding veterinarian, nor adopted by a band of drug-using rogues masquerading as a family.

The real story was much more exciting.

Catsby took me on a ride, back through the years to when he walked out of PetCo and hitchhiked across the country to meet Sir Catrick Stewart. His story was as epic in scope as *Lord of the Rings*, but with fewer lords and rings. I won't bore you with a play-by-play recap here, but suffice to say it was The Greatest Story Ever Told. Maybe if I were as talented an author as Nicholas Sparks, I could do it justice. A few of the highlights include his battle with the sasquatch in the foothills of South Dakota; the heated political debates in Missouri with the Republicans of Unusual Size (ROUS); being left for dead by the side of the road by a gang of Meow-

Nazis in a botched bank robbery in Bisbee, Arizona; etc. You get the idea.

I listened intently to his story as he acted all of this out. I didn't dare get up from my seat, even though my bladder was close to bursting for hours upon end. To break from his tale would be to break the spell. I was in this until the end. Finally, the fluids were too much for my body to handle. I simply let go.

Catsby glared at me. I could see at once that I'd erred. There was horror in his eyes, as if I'd just wet myself. Which, admittedly, I had.

"Continue," I said.

"I'll skip ahead to the end," he said, irritated. "I know it's late."

Catsby flashed forward to the iron gates of Paramount Studios in Burbank, California. The napping security guard paid this him no attention as he strolled through the gate.

The lot was a gritty, desolate wasteland, a post-apocalyptic concrete jungle populated by boxy warehouses, forklifts, and a few palm trees here and there that couldn't possibly be real. Even the usually sunny sky seemed to take on a gray pallor. He didn't see how they could film TV shows and movies here. It just didn't seem possible. Maybe the "magic" of television was literally magic—wouldn't that be something?

The roar of a great motor startled Catsby, and he leapt off the road just as a yellow 1922 Rolls Royce zoomed past. He had to be more careful. The irony of being hit by a car right at the end of a road trip was not lost on him, but that wasn't how he wanted his story to end. Car accidents are cheap narrative tricks, *deus ex machinas* pulled by authors too lazy to craft logical conclusions.

He didn't know what he was looking for. The *Enterprise*? Surely it had to be parked somewhere on the lot, perhaps in one of the warehouses doubling as a hangar. He hadn't been able to peek inside any of them, which meant this was a fool's errand—

Catsby stopped, his gaze fixed on the holy grail. No, it wasn't the starship, if there even was one. Maybe it was all a set. Who cared? This was even better. A row of ten trailers decorated with the Star Trek logo, presumably one for each of the lead and supporting actors. Nine of them were unremarkable, with names affixed to the doors he didn't recognize. The last trailer, however, made his heart race fast and furious: the captain's quarters.

But there was no one around. So what would Catsby do, he wondered? Hang out underneath the trailer until the star showed up? Who knew how long that would be, though. At the time, Catsby had no idea why filming was shut down for the day, nor how long it would be before it resumed again. Perhaps they were in between seasons. Perhaps (gasp) the series had been canceled. He would have read about that on one of the industry websites, wouldn't he? Well, yes, but remember that Catsby was a nomad back then, and didn't get onto the Internet that much. And when he did, he usually just clicked around at this or that, reading the headlines of the day. Catsby mulled over his options and decided to stay the night, and see what morning brought. Just as he was ducking under the trailer to hide out, a door flung open behind. He turned to see Sir Catrick Stewart, dressed in his red-and-black leotard, exiting a portable litterbox.

Stewart jumped at the sight of Catsby.

"Sorry," Catsby said. "This isn't what it looks like."

"It's not?" Stewart said after catching his breath. "Because it looks like you're trying to climb underneath my trailer."

"I...lost a ball under there?"

"You're a terrible liar. You're not the one who's been sending those weird, thirty-page handwritten letters, are you?"

"Letters? No, I've never written you before. I can't even hold a pen. Honest." Catsby held up his front paws.

"Damn. They were quite well written letters. Anyway, I get furries like you coming around all the time. You're not the first and you won't be the last. If you want an autographed headshot, though, give me your address and I'll have my agent mail you one."

Catsby lowered his head. "I don't have an address."

Stewart looked him over. "You're declawed and living on the streets? That's no easy task, I'll give you that. Are you hungry?"

Catsby nodded.

"Follow me," Stewart said, opening his trailer door. "We'll get you some tuna in you."

Inside, Catsby inhaled one can of tuna after another. When he wasn't chewing at a breakneck pace, he related his story to the actor. Unsolicited, of course, but the actor didn't interrupt. Instead, he nodded along, as if trying to absorb every detail.

"I need your help," Catsby said at the end of his tale. "You're one of the most respected actors working today, and you've done it while wearing a fursuit. When people look at you, they see a cat. When they look at me, I don't know what they see. Probably just a sad man in a costume."

"You're not bad, as far as furries go," Stewart said, removing his headpiece. Underneath, he was an old, bald man. Still handsome, but old and weary.

"People talk about furry space," Catsby said, "where they lose themselves in their fursona and forget they're a human being."

The teakettle on the stove let out a loud, long whistle. Stewart rose from his chair. "I'm familiar with the concept."

"Then tell me how to get there. No matter how long I wear this damned fursuit, no matter how long I crawl on all fours or go without speaking a word of English, I never seem to reach that plateau. I never *become* Jay Z. Catsby. I'm still—"

"Would you like some earl grey?"

Catsby shook his head.

Stewart poured the hot water over a tea bag and sat back down at the table in the middle of the trailer. "Do I look like someone who has disappeared completely into my fursona?" he asked, dipping the teabag. "What makes you think I'm not just a well-trained actor who occasionally wears a costume for film and television projects?"

"There's no filming going on today, and yet you're living in your trailer and using a litterbox. You can't fool me. This guise—the tea-drinking British actor—isn't who you are, not in your heart."

"You presume to know me."

"You can't hide your true self," Catsby said. "It's written all over your face."

Stewart laughed. His voice was as rich and as deep as advertised, and the trailer nearly shook with his laughter. "So it is. You want to know how I do it—how I wear the fursuit like a second skin," Stewart said. He ceased fiddling with the tea bag, and looked up and to the left, as if he was peering into the distant past. "You may not believe this, but I used to be a cat."

CHAPTER TWENTY-FIVE

"Once upon a time, I lived in a small cottage on a picturesque English hillside with an elderly woman. A cat lady," Sir Catrick Stewart said. "She rarely went anywhere, but when she did she'd bring back another cat with her. There had to be two dozen of us living under her roof. She kept us fed, albeit on dry food that the postman delivered once a week from Amazon. None of us had her full attention, even for a moment—which, for a cat, is a tough thing to handle. If we don't get enough attention, we get testy. Not a day went by that one of us didn't go wee on her mattress. I'm not proud of it, but I'll admit to having done it on occasion."

Catsby shuddered. He could barely imagine how bad things had gotten, that the only way to get someone to notice you was by urinating outside the litter box. And on their master's bedding! What a filthy way to conduct themselves—but, if what Stewart was saying was true, who could blame the poor animals?

"I couldn't live long in such a miserable household," Stewart said. "While I wasn't the put-together gentleman you see before you today, I had some sense that there was a future out there for me. I was only close to one of the cats there: Ian McKitten. We became fast friends, having entered the house only a few weeks apart. He had similarly refined senses. It didn't hurt that he was a bit of a looker. Together, we hatched a plan to leave the house of ill repute. We didn't know exactly what was beyond the doors of our poorhouse, but we had determination and we had claws. We would be free, and that was all that mattered.

"One day, when the old woman opened the door to receive her weekly supply of that crap she called food, Ian and I launched ourselves through her legs and out into the world. The gloriousness of our surroundings was almost too painful to behold—the sights, the smells….oh God, the smells. I paused and drew in a deep breath. I couldn't even identify half the smells tickling my nasal passageways…

"Ian snapped me back to my senses, just before the woman could scoop me up and drag me back inside. The postman, meanwhile, just stood there with this giant box in his hands, trying not to trip over us. The other cats watched from the windowsills. The blank expressions on their eyes chilled me to the bone. The bloody slaves. Most of them believed the woman was actually the captive. Can you believe such poppycock?

"Anyway, we ran. Four legs will carry you faster than two legs, and so we easily outran the woman. We had no real destination in mind, but we headed for the tall trees that marked the edge of the woods. There, we hoped to find cover under the brush."

Catsby shook his head. "You guys were crazy. What about all the other animals in the woods?"

Stewart shrugged. "We were young and dumb. We didn't think there was anything that could hurt us. After running for what felt like miles, we stopped to huddle under a fallen tree. The first thing we realized was that it was a lot colder than we'd expected, especially after the sun set. We huddled together for comfort, but didn't dare sleep. The howls of the wolves kept us awake. We were scared shitless. Literally. We defecated in the woods and did our best to cover it. We felt wild, untamed, and uncivilized. It was impossible to keep our coats clean, with all the dirt and grass and twigs sticking to us. One night in the woods, and we'd reverted to animals.

"You know—or maybe you don't—there's some debate in cat circles as to whether or not we lost or gained something by being domesticated by humans. Ian and I didn't want to go off the grid. Deep down, I think all we wanted was find another human to take care of us, one who would pay us the right amount of respect. One who wouldn't turn her house into some sort of feline tenement. Ian and I, we weren't revolutionaries. We weren't looking to overthrow the system.

We just wanted a little attention. Is that so much to ask?"

"Everybody wants to feel loved."

"Exactly," Stewart continued. "There are three things we all need: food, water, and tummy rubs. Much to my surprise, everything I'd been looking for was right there under my nose the entire time."

"Your mouth," said Catsby.

"Excuse me?"

"Your mouth is under your nose."

"Well, yes," Stewart said, "but I'm talking about Ian."

"You mean you two were..."

"Lovers. While I curled up with him to stay warm, it dawned on me why I'd been willing to go off on this crazy venture without the slightest thought to what would happen next. Because I was in love with Ian. As long as we were together, we could face down any obstacle. Ian's breathing grew deep and labored, and his heart beat faster; I assumed his mind was going to the same places mine was. I moved a paw down his tummy. He purred at my touch. Had he been thinking about this moment for months? Or had it taken him by surprise as well? Even though neither of us had our full wedding tackle, we still had urges. No, not urges—we had needs."

Sir Catrick Stewart's eyes glazed over. It was as if he'd been transported to another time and place. Catsby didn't want to be rude, but wasn't sure how much more he could listen to. And you, dear reader, may be worried we're about to get into a full cat-on-cat sex scene. Thankfully, Stewart sensed his guest's discomfort with the turn the story had taken, and moved on (thus saving you, dear reader, as well).

"After we finished our lovemaking, we dozed off—wolves and raccoons be damned," he said. "The afterglow of our lovemaking was too powerful to resist. When I next awoke, Ian was still asleep in my arms. I let out a massive yawn; not that I was tired, because I felt we'd slept until midday, judging by the position of the sun over our heads. Do you ever find that sometimes the sun just makes you yawn?"

Catsby yawned—not because of the sun, but because the story was dragging on and on, with no end in sight.

Stewart continued: "I slipped away from Ian, who was still sleeping. He was doing this little snoring thing he always did, which was just so adorably cute. I stretched my legs. What a perfect morning. The gray English skies were blue for a change. Bunnies were hopping, birds were singing, children were laughing. Okay, there weren't any children, but you get the picture. If there were children, they would have been laughing so hard that they'd have to be put down with tranquilizers. That's how beautiful it was.

"Leave it to me to screw it all up.

"There was this trail, you see, right next to the log. We hadn't noticed it at night, but there it was. I was hungry—and even more importantly, thirsty. Ian would be when he woke up as well. What if the trail led to water? I didn't see any other reason anyone would traipse through the woods, besides for food or water. It couldn't hurt to check it out. I doubted any dangerous animals would be on the prowl during the day. How incredibly naïve of me, for the most dangerous animal of all prowls during the day: man.

"The trail was not wide enough for horse nor car, but the grass was beaten down to the dirt. Perhaps it would lead to a house, where I could scrounge in the trash for a small meal. The thought of digging through garbage repulsed me, but we had to eat. After ten minutes without any luck, I was just about to give up when I found it: a cabin. Off to the side sat a trashcan. A peek into the aluminum trashcan couldn't hurt. And who knows? Maybe the owner of the house would be on the market for a pair of house cats. Wherever we ended up, we would end up together. It could be no other way.

"I approached the can with caution. Going by the overgrown lawn, the cabin might have been abandoned. Or maybe the homeowner just hated to do yardwork. I stood on my hind legs and nudged the lid. It was securely fastened. Of course it would be, out in the middle of the woods. I probably wasn't the first animal to get the idea to go after table scraps. Oh well. It had been worth a try.

"As I turned to walk back down the trail, the cabin door opened. A man in a blue cloak with a long, white beard emerged. It looked like he hadn't set foot outside in ages. Was this the male version of a cat lady? I froze.

In his right hand, he held a great wand with a brilliant scepter on the tip.

"'I am a great and powerful wizard,' the man said, his voice booming through the clearing. 'Anyone who follows my happy trail to my secret lair is granted three wishes. Therefore, I will grant thee three wishes.'

"Without thinking, I said I was famished and would like something to drink and eat.

"With a flick of his wrist, a lightning bolt shot out of the wand and struck the spot at my feet. Once the smoke cleared, I found a bowl of Meow-Mix Seafood Special and a bowl of water. I dove into the Meow-Mix, and before I knew it I'd finished off the entire thing. Then I washed it down by drinking my body weight in water. I rolled onto my back, feeling like a bloated American feline.

"I realized too late that I'd left nothing for Ian. My second wish, then, was for my friend to be fed as well. With another flick of his wrist, the powerful wizard shot another lightning bolt into the forest.

"I was down to one wish. I'd so far only thought with my stomach, and with my heart. I would need to think about this third wish. If I could have *anything* in the world, what would it be? Clearly, the one thing Ian and I wanted was to live in a household with someone who understood our needs. But it was clear that we understood each other's needs so well. We didn't need a person; we just needed each other. But a cat can't own another cat. Unless...

"'I want to be human, like you,' I began, 'and I want

my friend to be human as well, and I want to be able to speak like you, and walk like you, and—'

"The wizard stopped me. 'This sounds like more than one wish. You can't make multiple wishes, and just use the word 'and' to link them together. I'm giving you three wishes for free. I mean, you're not even paying for them.'

"I told him I didn't see what the big deal was. He was acting like a sore loser. I was well within my rights to use 'and' to string my wish on as long as I wanted. So what if the longer my wish was, the harder it was to fulfill? He shouldn't have offered in the first place. I didn't *ask* to be granted three wishes, after all.

"The wizard shook his head and let out a big sigh, but let me continue with my wish.

"When I finished, he asked if that was all—and I said yes, it was. Then with one last flick of his wrist, I was transformed by his magical wand into the man you see today."

"And Ian? What happened to Ian?"

Sir Catrick Stewart's countenance grew somber. "He was transformed as well. Unfortunately, the magical bolt responsible for his transformation also struck the dry brush where Ian had just finished eating the meal I'd wished for him to have—his last meal, as it turns out. A fire started, and the blaze consumed him alive. It was horrid, but it was over quickly."

"The wizard couldn't save him?"

"I was out of wishes. The wizard's power only worked when he was granting wishes. The wizard couldn't even save his own cabin from the blaze. The fire burned through the woods, and destroyed the cat lady's house. She lost her life—as did every cat inside. The horror...oh God, the horror.

"There's a saying: Be careful what you wish for. The truth of those words haunts me to this day. I lived for a while as a man, but couldn't escape my true nature. I was a cat, and am still a cat—the fursuit is irrelevant. That's why, unfortunately, I cannot help you."

Be careful what you wish for? The tragic ending to the tale would have turned any other furry away. But not Catsby. He had nothing to lose. If the wizard could transform Sir Catrick Stewart into a human being, then surely he could do the reverse.

Catsby stared into Stewart's eyes. "Where is this wizard now?"

CHAPTER TWENTY-SIX

"Stewart gave me a London address," Catsby said. "If you thought crossing the United States in a fursuit was rough, try crossing the Pacific Ocean."

"You mean the Atlantic Ocean?"

"I went the back way," he mumbled.

"So you found the wizard, and he transformed you."

Catsby shook his head. "The wizard had moved to New York. He was no longer in the business of granting wishes. No money in it. Instead, he'd become a stockbroker. You may have already guessed his name."

"Harry Potter."

"What? No. His name was Stratton Bellyflop. The Folf of Wall Street. He took me under his paw, and started me on the path to becoming the wealthy socialite you see before you today. He lived amongst animals in the woods for many years, and brought that experience to his furformance. He taught me how to become one with the animal within—and without. As you can see, there's no longer a dividing line between my persona and fursona."

"Wow," I said. "You swear on your mother's grave you're telling the truth this time?"

"I swear on her grave that the story I just told you is true. Or mostly true."

"What does 'mostly true' mean? Does that mean you embellished a few details for dramatic effect? Or that you made things up? Why can't you give me a straight answer?"

Catsby rolled his eyes and let out a great yawn. "Listen, Old Spice, it's getting late. I was born, and someday I'll die. What happens to us—to any of us—in between the first and last page of our lives is irrelevant."

"That's a bit of a cop-out. Anyhow, what are you trying to do now with Miley? She's married to a dog person. I know you're having fun with her and all, but you can't make her love you again. You can't repeat the past."

"Can't repeat it?" he said. "Of course you can!"

"No you can't," I said.

"Yes you can," he said.

"No you can't," I said.

"Yes you can," he said.

"No you can't," I said.

"No you can't," he said.

"Yes you—" I paused. "Okay, I see what you did

there, but the answer is still no. You can't repeat the past."

Catsby rose from his chair and looked out over the Atlantic Ocean, in the direction of his red light. In the direction of New York City. In the direction of his beloved. "I'm going to make everything better, like it was before. Miley will see. I'm not the same cat."

That, at least, I believed. He probably wasn't the same cat as when he'd first met Miley. It apparently hadn't crossed his mind, though, that she might have changed as well.

"What time do you think you'll sober up in the morning?" he asked.

I shrugged. "Noon or so," I said. Not that I ever really stopped drinking, even in my sleep.

He nodded. "I was wondering if you'd like to visit the Boobcannons in Park Slope in the afternoon. Miley's invited me over for lunch. Tucker will be there, and, well, you know."

Tucker would be there? I had a bad feeling about the whole setup, and told him as much.

"That's sort of why I'd like you to come with," he said, "in case there's any trouble."

If Tucker started pounding on Catsby, I wasn't sure I had the strength to pull him off—or pull Catsby out of harm's way. I preferred exercising my mind to my body, and thus had arms as big around as chicken fingers. On the other hand, Catsby had become my friend. He was also my employer and my landlord. I couldn't very well tell him no.

"I haven't been to Brooklyn in a while," I said. "It will be an adventure."

"That's the spirit, Old Spice. I'll see you around noon."

"I can see you right now," I said.

"So I can," he said. "Another thing: Looks like it's going to be a hot day—my personal weatherman says so, at least. Yessir. The hottest day of the year. Dress appropriately."

I hadn't met his weatherman yet, but there were many rooms in the house. I only saw his staff in passing. At some point during the summer, I started to see different people. "More trustworthy people," Catsby said. He wanted people who wouldn't gossip or sell his story to the papers. I assumed rumors had begun to circulate about him and Miley, which caused the turnover in staff. I wondered how many of these rumors had reached Tucker's cauliflower ears. I suppose we'd find out soon enough. If Catsby and Miley wanted a scene, they couldn't have picked a better day for one. The temperature was running high, and their tempers would certainly be running high as well. I had the distinct feeling that we were approaching not only the climax of the summer, but also the climax of the book I'd eventually write about it as well.

CHAPTER TWENTY-SEVEN

As we entered the Boobcannons' brownstone, I glanced up at Sir Catrick Stewart's window. The shades were drawn.

Miley hugged me. "Cordon's here," she whispered.

"Shoot me in the face with a firehose," I blurted. "I mean, uh, that's great."

Miley hugged Catsby, a little longer than seemed proper.

"Where's Tucker?" I asked nervously.

"On the phone, doing God knows what," Miley said.

Cordon was sprawled across the couch, reminiscent of my first visit to the Boobcannons'. "It's so hot, I can't move," she complained. "These stupid leather couches. You just stick to them in the summer. If I get up, my skin will peel off like a grape."

I smiled at her, but Cordon didn't return the smile. I was in the doghouse, for good reason. I heard Tucker's gruff voice in the kitchen. Sounded like he was arguing with someone.

"He's on the phone with his mistress," Cordon explained.

Miley pretended not to hear her comment; Catsby and I kept our mouths shut.

"Fine, then. Keep your damn book," Tucker shouted. "Could we talk about this later? I have company over... Some lunch date. Miley's cousin, I think."

"That bastard," Miley said. "Pretending he's talking to a rare book dealer. He hasn't read a book in his life."

"I don't know," I said. "I've visited his rare book dealer with him before. A little place in Williamsburg. A place called a 'bookstore.'"

"He's just full of surprises, isn't he?" Miley said sarcastically.

Tucker entered the room, strutting like a man with fifty-pound balls—by which I mean he appeared to be in great, cosmic pain. That's what kids will do to you.

"Dick," he said, shaking my hand. "How have you been?"

"Honestly? Or do you want me to lie?"

"You amuse me, Dick," he said with a laugh. His smile faded when he saw I wasn't alone. At the sight of Catsby, his eyes nearly popped out of their sockets like a pug's.

Tucker leveled a pointed finger at Catsby. "You...."

Catsby held his head high. Miley jumped between them. "Tucker, this is Jay—"

"We've met before. You invited this stray into my home?"

"Hey, now, I'm no stray—"

"Then where's your collar?"

Catsby said nothing. He was his own man—or cat, or whatever—as we could all plainly see. There was no reason for Tucker to take cheap digs at him, besides the fact that Catsby was spending more time with his wife these days than he was. Which is admittedly a very good reason to take cheap digs at someone.

"Let's calm down," Miley told her husband. "Catsby is a guest. Why don't you go grab some drinks for all of us?"

Tucker left the room, grumbling to himself. The second he was out of sight, Miley returned her attention to Catsby. "I love you," she whispered to him, loud enough for Cordon and me to overhear.

"Ahem." I didn't appreciate them drawing me into their little game. It was clear Tucker hadn't known Catsby would be coming over, and that they'd been planning the visit around my appearance all along. I used to be their third wheel back on the Jersey Shore; now I felt like the fourth or fifth wheel. By the end of the summer, I fully expected to be part of an eighteen-wheel semi. These people, I swear I couldn't even.

A nurse entered the room, leading a small girl by the hand.

"Mommy?" the child blurted.

Miley broke away from Catsby and stared at the child. "Tillie?"

"She wanted to see you," the nurse said.

"She's growing up so fast," I remarked.

The nurse nodded. "It's the gluten-free diet."

Miley reached her arms out and the child ran to her. They embraced. It was a touching moment...made all the more touching by Miley's later revelation that it was only the second time she'd actually met her daughter.

Cordon, meanwhile, started shaking on the couch. It appeared she was having a grand mal seizure. The nurse rushed to her side just as she wet herself. "She was complaining about the heat," I explained. The nurse slapped her in the face until she came around.

"I wish we could spend more time together," Tillie said, ignoring the medical emergency unfolding in the room. For a child, she was incredibly well spoken. A far cry from the idiot Miley wanted her to be.

"Are the boys not treating you well?" Miley asked.

"Boys mature at such a slow pace," Tillie said. "They're still in diapers."

"I'd love to wear diapers," I interjected. "Then I could drink all day without having to get out of bed."

Catsby shot me a dirty look. "We need to talk about your drinking later, Old Spice."

Tillie studied me. "Are you depressed?"

"It's nothing," I said, averting my eyes from the child. It was like she could see into my soul. She reminded me of one of those spooky children in horror films. If I looked into her eyes, I might catch fire.

Miley must have been creeped out too, because she

told the nurse to return Tillie to wherever the hell they kept the kid. A nursery? Under the stairs? I didn't want to know. I wanted to stay as uninvolved in Miley's affairs as possible, so that I wouldn't have to lie when I took the stand in her eventual trial for child neglect. As they say, ignorance is bliss.

Actually, that's a pretty wise thing to say. Whoever said it couldn't have been ignorant, and thus probably wasn't very blissful.

Once the child was gone, I relaxed again.

"What are we going to do this afternoon?" Miley asked. "And tomorrow, and the day after that—and every day for the next forty years?"

"Some of us don't have that long," Catsby said.

"What an awful thing to say," Cordon said, apparently recovered from her little episode.

"It's true, though. Cats don't live longer than twenty years."

Tucker returned with a cocktail shaker and some martini glasses, and began pouring out a neon-green liquid for us. It looked really girly, until I got a whiff of it and it singed my nose hairs off.

"This smells like anti-freeze," I said, taking a sip. "And it tastes like anti-freeze."

"That's because it is anti-freeze," Tucker said, handing out the rest of the glasses. "Drink up."

Catsby declined, sending Tucker into a frenzy. "What's the matter? Is this not fancy enough for you? Maybe I can find some milk in the fridge."

Catsby ignored the dig and asked for a glass of

water instead. Tucker left, seething with anger. The guy was a walking, talking car bomb.

"We could go into the city," Miley suggested.

"What happened to lunch?" I asked.

Miley glared at me. "Are you hungry? This heat has stolen my appetite. At least if we go into the city, we can find someplace with air conditioning."

"Yeah, I'd noticed you don't have central air," I said.

"Or window units," Cordon said, finally recovered from her little episode.

"Tucker says air conditioning is for pussies," Miley said. "Real men can withstand a little heat."

"Well this pussy needs to cool down," Cordon said, fanning herself in between her legs. As usual, that girl left nothing to the imagination. I wondered if I hadn't made a mistake by breaking things off with her. Surely I could buy a new charger for my phone. There had to be an Apple Store in New York City.

Tucker stormed back into the room with a glass of water in hand. He marched right up to Catsby and tossed it in his face. "How do you like that, you son of a bitch?"

Catsby patted his fur down, but didn't say anything.

"I'll go grab a towel," Miley said.

Tucker smirked, and set the glass on a side table. "I heard somebody talking about going to Manhattan. I'm game."

"Someone check the subway schedule," I said.

Tucker groaned. "I'd rather stick a glow stick up my ass than take public transportation."

"Do you do that a lot?" Catsby said coolly.

"Take public transportation? No."

"I was talking about the glow stick."

Tucker glared at him. "What I put up my ass is none of your business."

Miley returned and began toweling Catsby off. Tucker watched them with such intensity that I wondered if he wasn't going to shoot lasers out of his eyes and blow them both away. There could be no denying what was passing between Catsby and Miley. It was obvious to everyone in the room—even to Cordon, who was still in a daze. If they weren't lovers, they were the next closest thing: a pet and its owner.

"We're going to town," Tucker said, an evil glint in his eye. "We'll get a hotel."

"I have a room at the Times Square Hilton," Catsby offered. "It's a penthouse suite I use when I'm in town for business."

"Great," I said. "Should we call a taxi?"

"I've got a better idea," he said. "We'll take Citibikes."

"In this weather?" Miley asked.

"I think it will do us all some good," Tucker replied. "Exercise. When's the last time any of you got a workout in?"

"But we're positively hammered," Miley said. "You and your damned moonshine."

"We'll ride tandem Citibikes, then," Tucker said.

"I'll die—I'll positively *die*," Miley said.

Tucker scowled at her. She was the mother of his

children (sort of), but he probably wanted her to die for bringing a cat into his home. Let me be clear: I'm not suggesting he was capable of actually physically assaulting his wife. He's said many times he'd never lay a hand on a woman, and I believed him. But there are other ways to hurt someone, more insidious ways…like taking them bicycling in triple-digit weather. If his wife just so happened to die on the way to town, well, no sweat off his sack.

"It's okay," Cordon piped up. "I drove. My ride is parked around the corner."

"What about you guys?" Tucker asked, looking at Catsby and me.

"We took Catsby's helicopter, Charlie Tango," I said.

Tucker glared incredulously at Catsby. "You named your helicopter?"

Catsby shook his head. "I bought it in a fire sale from this tech guy out in Seattle. He was going through a rough divorce, and selling things left and right. It's parked on the roof right now."

Tucker looked up. "You can't just park a helicopter anywhere you like. Our roof isn't a helipad. It could—"

As if on cue, the helicopter crashed through the ceiling over the kitchen, smashing the table and chairs and sending all of us in the living room flying for cover. Once the dust cleared, we brushed ourselves off. Miraculously, no one had been harmed. You could see the clouds overhead through the hole in the ceiling.

"I've always wanted a skylight," Miley said.

Catsby started to say apologize, but cut him off before he could even get two words out. "I don't want to hear it. We'll deal with it later. Dick and I will grab a tandem Citibike. The rest of you ride in Cordon's car."

"It's not a car," Cordon said. "It's an Oscar Mayer Wienermobile."

CHAPTER TWENTY-EIGHT

"Did you catch all that?" Tucker asked over his shoulder, spitting out a small chunk of plaster. We were both pedaling the tandem, but were making very slow progress toward Manhattan. Tucker's impressive physique was all for show. When it came time to put it into action, he could barely move his bulky legs to pedal. This left me to do most of the work. I was positively hammered, and not that strong to begin with.

"Catch what? Charlie Tango falling through the roof?"

Tucker drew his lip up into a snarl. "That's not what I'm talking about. You all must think I'm some big dummy head. Some poo-pooing patootie. Maybe I am, but listen here: I have a kind of sixth sense when it comes to these things."

"You're a telepath."

"A what?"

"Like Professor Sex, in the *XXX-Men* movies. You can read minds."

He steered us out of traffic; we'd drifted too far into the road, and cars were honking at us. "You know I'm not into that super-hero junk. I don't need to be able to read minds to know that something's going on between this Catsby fellow and my girl. And I can tell by the way you reacted back there, you must have known the whole time."

"I live in the guy's house," I said. "Miley visits on occasion. I'm not privy to what goes on behind closed doors. It's none of my business."

Tucker grunted. "I looked into this furry. Hired a private investigator to dig into his background. And you know what I found?"

"You found that he's an Arizona man," I said with confidence.

"Is that what he told you? He didn't go to Arizona. He went to the University of Phoenix. That online college. He's nothing more than a two-bit hoodlum. A joker. A midnight toker."

My heart sank. Not an Arizona man?

"I'm not sure what kind of game he's playing," Tucker continued, "but he's going to lose."

"The road."

"The what?"

"Watch...the road," I said. My breathing had grown ragged. I felt like I was on the verge of another heart attack, like the time I'd mistaken cocaine for Stevia.

Tucker made a sharp right, and we careened down a side street. "This isn't the way to Manhattan," I said.

Tucker didn't say anything. Instead, he continued to steer us through the side streets. I pedaled to keep us moving, without any idea where we were headed. The full beards and rainbow-puking unicorn tattoos, however, clued me in to our location.

"What are we doing back in Williamsburg?"

"Going to see a friend," Tucker said.

"A girlfriend?"

"What's it to you?"

"We're already going to be an hour late to Manhattan because someone's not helping with the pedaling," I said. "We don't have time for a booty call."

"We have time for whatever I want," Tucker said.

We cruised to a stop at Books and More. We dismounted, and leaned the bike against a lightpost. The bike fell over, smashing into the cement. I tried to right the bike, but Tucker dragged me away. "It's just a rental," he said. I made a mental note never to lend anything to Tucker.

Inside the store, Harper greeted us with a small nod. His skin was pale and clammy, like a guy on a month-long bender. In other words, he looked like I probably did. Just another reason not to look in a mirror.

(The other reason I've never looked in a mirror is I'm afraid my reflection won't appear and that's how I'll know that I'm a vampire. I would rather be confined to some underground hell with the Devil whipping me on a St. Andrew's cross for eternity than walk the Earth, unaware of my own unbeating heart.)

"I need to talk to Lima," Tucker said.

"She's in the back," Harper said, his voice as weak as his body. "You know where to find her. Are you going to buy that first edition finally? We really need the money."

"If you need money, you should get into another line of work," Tucker said.

"Funny you should say that—we're trying to sell the store. Get out of town for a while. Go west, maybe. Or east. I'm not too good with directions."

"That's insane! Who moves out of the city? There's nothing out there," Tucker said, waving his hand. "I went to school in the Midwest. You don't know how empty the heartland is."

"We'll find someplace." Then, in a low whisper, Harper added, "I think Lima's seeing someone behind my back. If we leave town, things will be like they were back in the old days. Maybe we'll fall in love again."

"We'll see about that," Tucker said, stomping to the backroom. I shifted my weight, and wiped the sweat off my brow. It occurred to me that Harper had no idea the suspected cuckold was right under his nose. The man was booksmart, but lacked common sense. I could empathize.

"How long have you owned the store?" I asked, attempting to dispel the awkward silence.

"About ten years."

"So you remember the time B.A."

His eyes glazed over. "Before Amazon? Yeah. You look a little young."

"I'm twenty-two," I said, "the last time I checked."

"Then you probably don't remember what it was like. There used to be bookstores on every block. Now, they're all payday loan places. We're one of the last bookstores in New York—hell, one of the last in the country. It's time to hang up the reading glasses, though."

"Isn't this place called 'Books and More'? Surely, you could just sell more of the more."

He frowned. "The 'more' stands for 'more books.'"

"That's unfortunate."

The bookstore cat raced past me and under the counter. Tucker followed shortly thereafter, fuming. "Let's go, Dick."

We hopped back on our Citibike. Tucker didn't tell me what Lima had said, but it was clear she was leaving town with her husband. Tucker was now faced with the prospect of losing not only his wife, but also his mistress. I sensed the anger and confusion broiling in his mind like our skin under the midday sun. I half-expected his head to explode into flames like Ghost Rider. I didn't dare mention this to Tucker; I didn't want to be subjected to a half-hour lecture on the nerds' takeover of pop culture. I wasn't going to defend the Nicolas Cage *Ghost Rider* films. No way. Nicolas Cage is a personal hero of mine, but those films were flaming bags of dog doo.

CHAPTER TWENTY-NINE

An hour later, we arrived at the Hilton. Cordon's Wienermobile was already parked out front. Tucker rolled the bike into traffic.

We took the elevator straight to the top of the hotel. Tucker tried to act nonchalant when Cordon let us in, but he couldn't hide the jealousy in his eyes. The penthouse suite was large and ostentatious. I hadn't expected anything less from Catsby.

"I thought we would just go to the movies," I said, marveling at the opulent palace, which included a hot tub and single-lane bowling alley. This place put Tucker's little dead-celebrity flop house to shame. One of the lesser Hilton sisters was behind a counter, ready to rent us bowling shoes at the drop of a hat. If anyone literally dropped a hat, someone would probably hop out of a closet to pick it up.

"There's a movie theater in the next room," Catsby said.

"You sure they allow pets in this place?" Tucker asked.

Miley emerged from the bathroom. "You guys finally made it. I was beginning to think you got lost."

"I'm a man," Tucker said, jacking up the bass in his voice. "I don't get lost."

"Unless you're looking for the clitoris," Cordon said, giving me an evil eye.

This was true, but my excuse—a good one—was that she was in need of a trim. It was like looking for bigfoot in the Pacific Northwest.

"Where's the booze?" Tucker asked, his voice brimming with irritation.

"Calm down, Old Spice—we'll phone the concierge and have a few bottles—"

"Don't 'Old Spice' me. Where'd you pick that up, anyhow?"

"I can call you something else, if you'd prefer—but I doubt you'd like it any better."

Miley jumped between them once again. "You two! If this turns into a big brouhaha, I'll leave at once. There's no need to fight."

Catsby phoned the concierge. Meanwhile, Tucker and Miley faced off with each other like they were about to fight or make love. There's such a thin line between emotional extremes, it's hard to tell sometimes.

"So you're an Arizona man," Tucker said without looking in Catsby's direction. I strolled to the window and looked out onto Times Square, which was as gaudy and packed as ever. What a beautiful, revolting city.

"That's correct," Catsby said.

"Let's hear about it...Old Spice."

Catsby cleared his throat. "I was enrolled in a few online classes at the University of Phoenix, which is headquartered in Phoenix, Arizona. I never graduated, though, so there's not much to talk about."

Tucker glanced around the room to gauge our reactions to this ho-hum revelation.

"You may look at me and assume I've always been well off, but that's not the case," Catsby said. "I worked at Starbucks for a while, and they paid my tuition at the University of Phoenix. I was let go when the tough times came, so that was the end of my education. I could go back anytime I wanted, but what's the point? It's like one of those little old ladies who finishes her associate of arts degree on her deathbed. Pointless for someone like me who has it all."

"You have it all," Tucker said. It wasn't a question. It was an accusation.

Before Catsby could answer, there was a knock at the door.

I answered. A waiter was standing there with a couple bottles of rum. I snatched them and slammed the door.

"I have one more question for you, Mr. Catsby," Tucker said, a crazed look in his eyes. Actually, it was the same crazed look that he'd had all day.

"You want to get Reddit up in here?" Catsby asked. "Go ahead: ask me anything."

"Just what do you think you're doing with my wife?"

Cordon and I exchanged a terrified look that said, "YIKES."

Miley covered her face and started sobbing.

"I suppose the latest rage is to sit around and do nothing while your wife runs around with some strange cat," Tucker continued. "Is that it? Do family values mean nothing? Oh, how I wish for the good ol' days when wives actually obeyed their husbands. Doesn't anyone read the Bible anymore?" Tucker flung his words around the room with such venom that I reflexively ducked when he looked my way. He was speaking nonsense, like a Fox News anchor with a broken teleprompter.

"You haven't read the Bible," Miley said, tears streaming down her face. "You watched the TV miniseries, and said that was more than enough."

Tucker glared at her. "I know I don't throw big parties like your friend here. Is that what it is? Sorry that I don't want to invite every Tom, Dick, and Harry into our home." Tucker turned to me. "No offense, Dick."

I shrugged. I tossed back a glass of straight rum, and poured myself another.

"I'm going to tell you something, OLD SPICE," Catsby said.

Tucker leaned back and crossed his arms. "Oh, this

is going to be good." I passed him a drink. He downed it in one gulp. Neither of us was going to be in any condition to bike home.

Catsby cleared his throat. "Miley's not in love with you. She's never loved you."

"You're insane!" Tucker screamed. "You think she loves *you*?"

"She'd never have married you, if I'd had the means to support her when we first met."

"When you first met? You mean this has been going on since before college?"

Catsby nodded. "And another thing—"

Tucker cut him off. "I want to hear it from her. Miley? Is this true?"

Miley slid down onto the floor, where she curled up into a ball. In between sobs, she said—over and over—"Yes, yes, yes."

Tucker balled his fists up and faced Catsby. "You've been screwing my wife?"

Miley looked up. "Whoa. Hold on. Time out."

All eyes were on her.

"We've never had sex," she continued. "That's disgusting. I mean, he's a cat...and I'm a person. I just pet him. Scratch him behind the ears. That sort of thing. For God's sake, he doesn't even have testicles."

I winced and felt my sack tighten. Catsby turned away from everyone, embarrassed at the revelation.

"Well isn't this a turn of events!" Tucker shouted, pleased with himself. The anger had disappeared from his voice. Instead, he sounded downright jovial. "Do you still love me?" Tucker asked his wife.

Miley shrugged. "Whatevs."

"Good enough for me," Tucker said.

"I want to speak with her alone," Catsby said, finding his voice again.

"Go for it," Tucker said. "Why don't you two go for a long drive and talk about your precious little feelings. She's not leaving me, you know. Not for some feline hustler."

"Hustler?" Miley asked. "I thought you were on the up-and-up."

"Go ahead, Catsby—tell her all about your little pyramid scheme."

"It's not a pyramid scheme," he began. "It's called Amway—"

Miley stared at him blankly, as if he'd just told her he'd murdered one of her children. He began telling Miley his story, his real story, denying all the allegations about his dealings and trying his best to clear his name. It was obvious to us all that it wasn't working. Not this time. She drew further and further away from him. His words were hitting her ears, but not being processed by her brain. Which, honestly, happened quite a bit with Miley.

When it sounded like Catsby had reached the end of his sob story, Tucker excused them. "Why don't you both head out now. Get a headstart on us."

Cordon tossed her keys to Catsby. "Take my ride. You guys can have some privacy."

"Go ahead," Tucker said with a nod of approval. "And on your way back to Brooklyn, maybe you can explain to my wife what a 'furry' is."

"A furry?" Miley asked.

"We can talk about it in the car," Catsby said, ushering her out the door. They left without saying goodbye, like Batman. I looked around the room, unsure which of us was Commissioner Gordon and which of us was Robin. The likely answer was none of us. We were all Jokers, Riddlers, and Penguins. Maybe Cordon was Catwoman, though—I could see her filling out a leather catsuit nicely.

"Wait," Cordon said. "Did she really think he was a cat this entire time?"

Tucker just shrugged, as if to say, "That's my wife for ya."

I breathed a sigh of relief. All things considered, it felt like we'd narrowly avoided a tragedy. Catsby's heart had been crushed, of course, but there are plenty of ways to remedy a broken heart. Alcohol. Time. More alcohol. My point is that it wasn't the end of the world. Although we'd ended the day on a bittersweet note, it could have been a lot worse. I'd fully expected someone to be killed!

Little did I know, that's exactly what was about to happen. If you're looking for a happy ending, put this book down and visit a massage parlor. The shit's about to hit the fan, boys and girls.

CHAPTER THIRTY

The Wienermobile didn't stop. It came roaring out of the darkness, bouncing down on the narrow Brooklyn street like an out-of-control Macy's Thanksgiving Day balloon. Another car, one following the Wienermobile, stopped after the accident. The driver rushed to the victim's aid, but it was too late. Their life had been snuffed out like a late-inning Cubs rally.

Cordon, Tucker, and I were on our way back to Park Slope when we came upon the scene. As our taxi rolled past the flashing lights of a pack of emergency vehicles, something compelled Tucker to ask the driver to stop. At first I worried he wanted to have another word with his mistress, since we close to Books and More. But then I realized, with horror, that he must have recognized the distinctive shape of the horse mask under the black tarp.

Tucker leapt out of the cab and rushed to the scene

of the accident. I instructed Cordon to wait with the driver, and followed Tucker. I found him attending to Lima. She was hovering over the draped corpse, shaking and crying.

"The limp bastard!" she cried. "He didn't even slow down."

"What happened here?" Tucker asked. "What bastard?"

"He's dead. Dead!"

Tucker frowned at the body on the ground. "Who's dead, Lima?"

"Harper."

A grizzled-looking cop approached us, clipboard in hand. "Who saw what happened? We're taking statements."

"I saw it," Lima said. "I'm his wife."

Not anymore, I thought grimly.

"What was your husband doing in the middle of the street?" the cop asked.

"We were just having some fun in the bedroom. He put my horse mask on. I don't know what happened, but he went...wild. Untamed. He ran out of our apartment and into the street."

"You saw the car that did this?"

"It wasn't a car. It was a hot dog. A giant hot dog. When the driver saw Harper, he just stepped on the gas and ran through him."

"Hot dog?" the cop asked. "What kind? Polish sausage, kielbasa...."

"I don't know. Just a friggin' hot dog!"

"In a bun? Did it have ketchup and mustard, or was it Chicago style—mustard only?"

"Why is this important?" Tucker snapped. "Her husband has died, and you're asking whether there was any ketchup on the car that killed him. How many Wienermobiles could there be in Brooklyn?"

The cop gave him an icy stare. "Wienermobile? I didn't hear the lady call it a Wienermobile."

Tucker scrambled for an answer. "No? Well, I just assumed. It's the only hot dog you can drive that I've ever heard of."

The cop eyed Tucker and me with suspicion. "Either of you see the accident?"

We shook our heads.

"Then move along. This is no place for gawkers."

Tucker nodded, and whispered something to Lima. Her eyes lit up, but she didn't say a word.

We headed back to the taxi. "What did you say to Lima back there? Did you tell her we know the driver?"

"I hated her husband more than anybody, but he didn't deserve to die." Tucker opened the cab's door for me. "I may have dropped a few hints as to the driver's identity."

"I thought it was over between you and Catsby."

"It will be," he said. "Soon."

CHAPTER THIRTY-ONE

"Miley must be home," Tucker said, eyeing the light on in their bedroom window. The front door was unlocked. Tucker paused before stepping inside. "Sorry, Dick, I should have kept the taxi around to take you back to Jersey. If you're going back there, that is. After what Catsby did..."

"I doubt he'll be there. He's probably halfway to Mexico by now."

Cordon rolled her eyes. "Oh, please. He's got money. He'll buy his way out of this."

"Maybe so," I said. "Let's just wait until we hear his side of the story first before passing judgment."

"Always the sensible one, aren't you?" Tucker said. "You're both welcome to stay here. The helicopter destroyed our guest bedroom, but we have a couch. You'd have to share..."

I faced Cordon, who smiled back at me. It was

tempting—there seemed to be a slight chance at reconciliation—but, ultimately, I felt compelled to return to Catsby's. If he was there, I had to let him know the clock was ticking.

"Thanks, but I think I'll go for a walk, and then head back to Jersey," I said.

Cordon seemed disappointed, but she planted a goodnight kiss on my cheek. Tucker grunted his goodbye, and they disappeared inside. I walked to the street corner, where a familiar furry figure leapt out at me from behind a stoop.

"It's me," Catsby said.

"Of course it's you. Who else would it be?" I glanced back at the Boobcannons' apartment. "What are you doing out here? Where's the Wienermobile?"

He said nothing.

"That bookseller is dead, you know."

"So it wasn't a horse," Catsby asked.

"It wasn't a horse," I repeated.

"And it wasn't ketchup on the fender, either."

I flinched. "Where'd you park?"

"The Wienermobile? It's in the East River."

"There's a parking garage in the middle of the East River?"

"No, Old Spice," he said. "The Wienermobile is at the bottom of the river."

Cordon wasn't going to be too happy about this turn of events. From what I recalled, she still owed taxes on it after winning it in the Fourth of July hotdog eating competition.

"How did the accident happen? It was an accident, wasn't it?"

"Of course," he said. "I tried to grab the wheel, but she slapped me away. I don't know what she was thinking."

"You don't mean...oh God. Miley was driving?"

"Women drivers," he said, shaking his head. "You know what I'm saying?"

"Women drivers," I said, nodding in agreement. "I know what you're saying."

(Let the record show that I later checked the Internet for the statistics, and women are actually safer drivers compared to men.)

"I'm not going to tell anyone she was driving," Catsby said. "Keep that between us. I'll take the blame."

"You'll be arrested. You won't last a day in prison in that fursuit."

"They'll have to catch me first. I'll fly to some country like Switzerland or Russia. I'll tell them I'm a hacker or something, and that the U.S. government is after me."

"Then what are you doing out here? Get going!"

He stared at the illuminated window down the block. "I'm waiting for Miley. She said she'd ask her husband for a divorce. Tell him it's over, that she's taking the kids. She's coming with me."

I laughed outloud. I suppose I shouldn't have done that, but c'mon. Was he serious?

"You head home," he said, ignoring my ejaculation.

"I'm waiting here."

"How long?"

His frown had never looked more serious. "As long as it takes."

I wanted to say something more, but there was nothing else to say. I headed toward a main thoroughfare to hail a cab. There was no way Miley was going to go anywhere with Catsby. We'd all seen the distant look in her eyes when he tried to explain himself to her. She may have loved him, once upon a time, but that time had long since passed. The past couple of months had been little more than a coda, a movie tacked onto the end of a canceled TV series. They'd had their *Serenity*. It was all over for them now.

CHAPTER THIRTY-TWO

The moment I returned to Catsby's mansion, I passed out in the foyer. It had been a long day, and maybe I'd had a few more drinks at a bar on the Shore. Maybe. That's the thing about blackouts: you don't remember what exactly caused them. You just wake up the next morning on the linoleum in a puddle of sweat and tears.

I glanced at the television in his living room, but didn't turn it on. Surely the murder would be all over the news, but the last thing I wanted to do was relive the horror. I showered and changed. On my way back downstairs, the front door opened. Catsby walked in. Alone. His grumpy expression somehow looked sadder in the early morning light.

"Where's Miley?" I asked. I knew damn well where she was: with her husband.

"She just needs more time," Catsby said, slamming

the door. "She just needs to sort things out with Tucker."

"You should leave the country, then. Get a head-start. I'll let her know where you're at, and she can join you later."

He hopped into an empty refrigerator box he liked to sulk in from time to time. "I'm not leaving without her, Old Spice," he said, his voice muffled by the cardboard.

The doorbell rang. He poked his head up.

"The police," I said. "Head out the back door. I'll stall—"

He leapt out of the box with surprising speed for a man in a full-body costume. "What if it's not the police? What if it's Miley?"

Catsby threw the door open—

The gunshots rang throughout the mansion, echoing in the halls. I dropped to the floor, covering the back of my neck like I was in the middle of a sharknado drill at school. I think I might have wet myself, but when wasn't I wetting myself that summer? The shooting continued—six shots in all, according to the police report. Catsby's body careened backward and landed in a heap next to me. I didn't hear him hit the tile. My ears were ringing. It all seemed to happen in slow motion, like a Zach Snyder movie. It was equally as violent.

When the shooting stopped, I glanced up and saw the murderer, smoking gun still in hand.

Lima.

She appeared to be in a trance. I raised my palms to indicate surrender. I was slowly getting to my feet when I felt something whisk over my head. The next thing I knew, a throwing star was stuck in Lima's forehead.

She fell forward and landed on top of Catsby. I turned my head to see the butler striking a karate pose, his legs spread and bent, his arm still extended after releasing the throwing star. We both paused a beat, catching our breath from the excitement.

Together, we rolled Lima's body off Catsby. His orange fursuit was stained bright red, matted down with her blood. There weren't any visible bullet holes in Catsby's costume, but there was no doubt he'd been hit multiple times—blood had soaked through his backside and was pooling underneath him. I rolled him onto his side, frantically running my hands through his wet fur in search of a zipper.

There wasn't one.

"How do we get him out?" I asked.

"We don't."

"There has to be a zipper or something. What do you do when he takes a shower?"

He rolled Catsby onto his back again. "It's sewn on, Mr. Narroway. The only openings are in the headpiece and down below, for using the toilet."

I stared at Catsby's open eyes—not the big anime eyes that were glued onto his headpiece, but his real, human eyes visible through the slits beneath the cartoon eyes. His real eyes were lifeless. I reached a finger in and closed each of them, putting the man I knew as Jay Z. Catsby to rest. If he had nine lives, he'd spent them all.

CHAPTER THIRTY-THREE

The firemen were the first on the scene, attending to the victims. They rushed to my side as well, since I was covered in blood—and discovered, much to my surprise, that I'd been shot through the gut. A stray bullet had gone clean through me. I was still so drunk from the night before that I hadn't felt a damn thing. As they loaded me onto a stretcher, I saw the firemen cutting Catsby's fursuit off. I closed my eyes. There are some things I don't have the stomach to watch, like Hulk Hogan's sex tape.

As I recovered in the hospital for the second time that summer, the media had a field day with the killings. They say journalists are unbiased. Ha. We all have biases. Journalists, by and large, must be dog people. That's the only possible explanation for the slanted coverage. Jay Z. Catsby's mug was plastered on the front page of the *New York Post*, alongside Lima and Harper's. The headline: "CAT SCRATCH FEVER."

They made Catsby out to be the villain, dragging his good name through the mud. (They also dug up his real name, which I won't repeat out of respect for the dead.) What kind of monster could run someone down with a Wienermobile and not even stop, they asked? The answer, everyone agreed, was plain as day: a monster who'd been hiding his real face all along, because underneath lurked a heartless psychopath.

Catsby's name could have easily been cleared, if Miley had come forward and admitted she was driving that fateful night in Williamsburg. Detectives interviewed every one of us who'd been at the Times Square Hilton with Catsby. None of us revealed the truth; I doubt Tucker or Cordon even knew the truth. I couldn't turn my own cousin in, and Miley, for her part, kept her mouth shut. Who could blame her? It was an open and shut case, as far as the police were concerned. Catsby looked guilty as hell, sinking the Wienermobile in the East River. No one would ever have to know the truth…unless, on the off chance, this book is published and Miley is still alive. (Sorry, Miley!)

The police talked to me multiple times in the hospital. Or maybe I should say they "interrogated" me. Was I really in charge of Catsby's finances? Did I know how he made his money? I told them everything I knew: he was an independent business owner. An "I.B.O." in Amway lingo. I apologized about the mess I'd left in his office. Once they figured out I couldn't even add two and two together, they decided I was being straight with them.

I learned from a TV exposé why they were so interested in the details of Catsby's operation. Amway was just a cover for Catsby's real business: organ trafficking. Hearts, livers, lungs, and kidneys. He and his business associate Stratton Bellyflop were in charge of a vast network of organ harvesters. The thieves cut organs out of the living and recently deceased, and sold them on the black market. There was a good chance that one of their operatives had stolen my kidney earlier in the summer. Not only that, but the organ I'd received as a transplant may have very well been my own.

I was angry for a few days about this. Pissed off, even. However, Catsby was dead. What's the point in holding a grudge against the dead? You can yell at them all you want, but they're not going to hear you. (Unless there's such a thing as ghosts, in which case I might reevaluate my position.) There was no denying that Catsby had most likely caused me excruciating, unimaginable pain. But, at the end of the day, I had my kidney back. He must have known he'd been the cause of my misfortune, because he'd been so willing to give me a transfusion using his own blood. He picked me up when I was down, and gave a roof over my head. Otherwise, what would I have done when the AirBnB I was renting burned down? Called my parents and asked for more money, probably.

With the beating Catsby's name took in the press, it was no surprise that the public turned against him. The thousands of revelers who'd frequented his parties earlier in the summer had abandoned him. I blamed most of this on the Folf of Wall Street, who had no doubt introduced Catsby to this gruesome organ-trafficking business that he'd gotten caught up in. Stratton Bellyflop was sitting in jail, awaiting his own day in court.

After six days in the hospital, I was discharged. This time, there was no car out front waiting for me. I wasn't even sure if I had someplace to live. Had the feds seized all of Catsby's property, including his mansion?

I arrived at the old Catsby place late in the evening. Weeds were already beginning to overgrow the property. If I'd told you the place hadn't been inhabited in years, you would have believed me. I mean, basically, I can tell you anything and you have to believe me—I'm the narrator. That's right. You have no choice but to rely on me. You can always look up everything I'm saying online if you wanted to, so I guess that keeps me honest. Or so you hope.

Anyhow, the front door was locked. I didn't have a key on me. Nothing under the welcome mat, either. I rang the bell a couple of times, hoping the butler or the weatherman or any one of his many other servants might answer. Silence.

I crept to the back of the house. The yacht was still docked on the beach. Since I had nowhere to stay for the night, and no one else was using it, why not lay out on one of the chairs on its deck? I walked out on the dock, the wooden planks creaking under my feet.

Everything had fallen apart, it seemed—all within less than a week's time.

The same could be said for a person: if we don't take care of ourselves, we're liable to fall into disrepair at an alarmingly fast rate. Getting shot had been a godsend for me. I'd sobered up while in the hospital, and could see that my drinking had been out of control. As I've said before, it was a symptom of the post-Great Recession era—and I was sick of it. Sick of it all. Thanks, Obama. I was ready to go back to the Midwest, back to my parents' house and return to my books. I hadn't read anything all summer, except for the fanfiction at my job. Forget the knockoffs; I was ready to read real books again.

Once onboard the boat, something out on the water caught my eye. Something dancing. Something red. It flitted around, sometimes in circles, sometimes in figure eights. It disappeared, only to reappear seconds later in another spot—closer. No, further....

Catsby's red light.

"Come to pay your final respects?"

I swiveled around to see the butler on the deck behind me. He must have been in the cabin when I boarded. He was holding something small and silver in his right hand. At first glance, I thought it was a knife because of the way the moonlight reflected off its surface. He pointed it at me, and a red dot appeared on my chest. The butler twirled his wrist, and the red dot danced.

"The red light was—"

"A laser pointer?" he said, clicking it off. "To you and me, yes. To Catsby, it was so much more. It represented Ms. Boobcannon; it represented them together, happy at last with a litter of their own. The red light was his future, just always out of his paws. He would stare at it for hours. We'd even boat out after it on occasion, but the closer we got, the further away it seemed. Poor guy. I don't think he ever figured out it was a laser pointer. I didn't have the heart to tell him."

The red light had remained the perfect metaphor, right to the very end. It was nothing more than a cheap illusion, a servant's trick on his master. Even in Catsby's final moments, he believed in a future where he and Miley lived together, and she gave him all the scratches and pets he desired—and he gave her all a cat could give an owner.

I was still a little confused on that last point. What do cats do for their owners, exactly? They're not their best friends; they're not dogs. They entertain them, I suppose, but equally aggravate and disdain their owners. It's a contract we enter into willingly! That's the craziest part about owning a cat. And yet, despite my bad experience with the pet dragon, I wouldn't have minded owning a cat. I suppose I couldn't shake that dream, the one I'd had since reading the bowdlerized version of *Huck Finn*.

"So what do we do now?" I asked.

The butler leaned back in his reclined chair. "There's the funeral tomorrow. If you want to pay your last respects tonight, before the media circus, the back door to the house is unlocked. The casket's in the living room."

Inside the abandoned house, I flipped the light switch. Nothing. The power company must have cut the electricity. Thankfully, there was enough moonlight streaming through the picture windows to illuminate my way. You know what they say about living in glass houses: They have great natural lighting.

In his living room, I found the casket sitting on a table. The lid was open. Moonlight streaked across it, and I could see Catsby's nose poking out above the casket. After a long pause, I crossed the room cautiously, quietly, as if I was worried about waking the dead.

Up close, my former employer didn't look that different from when he'd been living. His trademark frown was still there. The coroner had washed the blood out of his fursuit. In death, his orange fur had a radiant sheen that had been lacking in life, like it had been steamcleaned. It's disturbing when someone looks better in death than they ever did in life. The most unnerving aspect, however, were the plastic eyes. They were wide open and as cartoonish as ever. They were glued onto the headpiece, of course, so I don't know if they had any option. But still.

"You poor son of a bitch," I said under my breath.

That's when I felt something brush against my right leg.

I looked down.

A tabby.

I knelt to get a closer look at the cat. During all my time at Catsby's, I'd never seen an actual cat. Maybe it had snuck in when the casket was being delivered. In any case, the cat's orange complexion and frown were...strikingly familiar. I stroked its back, and it purred his approval. "What do you say we get out of here, little guy?"

He cocked his head, as if considering the question. I opened my arms wide. He hopped willingly into my clutches. I held him tight to my chest as he continued purring. Maybe there was a little girl crying somewhere over her lost cat, but that wasn't my concern. He didn't have a collar, so he was mine now. Finders keepers, losers weepers.

"Just you and me, buddy. We'll go wherever we want. Leave this wretched place behind. I'll call my parents, and have them add some more money to my bank account. We'll spend as much time as we want cruising across the country—like Jack Kerouac. And you can be whoever the other guy was in *On the Road*. Actually, scratch that. We'll take the yacht. Our next adventure shall be...*On the Boat*."

The cat stared up at me with his big, brown eyes. He could probably tell already that our road trip would turn out less Kerouac and more Mad Max.

"You need a name, don't you? Considering the circumstances, I think I'll call you...Jay Z. Catsby the Second."

Catsby purred in delight.

We returned to the boat. I woke the butler, who said

he would be delighted to cruise the world with us. As he untethered the boat, I scanned the horizon. For a second, I thought I could see the blinking red light—but no, the butler had put his laser pointer away. There was nothing out there. Nothing but time, and distance, and the years that would recede before us like my father's hair and his father's before him.

"We're all ready," the butler said.

I took the wheel, Catsby perched on my shoulder. I turned the key in the ignition and the yacht started up. I'd never piloted one before, but how different could it be than driving a car?

So we beat on, our boat against the current, borne back ceaselessly into the shore....

CHAPTER THIRTY-FOUR

When I said we were "borne back ceaselessly into the shore," I wasn't trying to be poetic. What I meant is that we crashed on the rocky shoreline just a few miles south of the dock. Driving a boat was probably as easy as driving a car, but I'd forgotten something very important: I'd never driven a car. I'd always had roommates or public transportation or parents. My bad.

The boat splintered into millions of pieces. It happened so fast. Catsby and I plunged into the Atlantic Ocean. We were underwater for what felt like minutes. Although we miraculously surfaced together, our ordeal wasn't over: we'd been swept out to sea. I immediately worried that we'd be attacked by a shark or a giant squid, but remembered that all marine life was extinct due to pollution.

Unfortunately, drowning was still a distinct possibility. I latched onto a passing piece of debris—the door to the cabin. I placed Catsby on it, while I treaded water. Catsby shook himself off and stared at me, as if to ask when I would be joining him on the door. I shook my head. There wasn't enough room on it for both of us.

"We'll make it," I said, shivering. Despite the record temperatures we'd been experiencing, the sea was a cold bitch in the dead of night. "It'll be a few minutes, but someone will be here."

I couldn't be sure—it could have been nothing—but I thought I saw a small tear ran down Catsby's face.

"Don't you do that," I said. "Don't say your goodbyes now. You're going to live. You'll go on to make kittens and watch them grow up. You'll die an old cat, warm in your cat bed. You hear me, Catsby?"

He cocked his head, as if to suggest he was indifferent to what I was saying. Perhaps he—like all cats, I suppose—didn't understand English. How I wished my dearly departed furry friend was still around to bridge the gap! Maybe he didn't really speak to cats; maybe it was just another of his outlandish stories. His palace of lies had come crumbling down. If he'd still been around, I wouldn't have been drifting at sea anyway.

"Promise me you'll live. Promise me you won't let go."

I reached a hand out to Catsby. He made no move to put his paw into my hand. Instead, he lapped at the fur on his stomach. He started hacking almost immediately, and spit up a wet hairball in my face.

"I love you too," I said, wiping it away.

We drifted along the choppy sea for a while—minutes or hours, I don't know. How long could I tread water? Even if I were strong enough to swim, it wouldn't have been of any use. I couldn't even see the shore in the darkness, so wouldn't have even had any idea what direction to swim in.

We bumped into something. The butler's lifeless body. I'd never even learned his name. Or maybe he told me, and I'd just forgotten it. Maybe he didn't have to die in vain. I pulled his floating corpse closer, and patted down his pant pockets. I felt something long and cylindrical.

I pulled out the laser pointer and breathed a sigh of relief.

I could shine it into the night sky. Somebody would have to see it. I pressed the button on its side and an explosion of red light shot straight up into the air, cutting through the darkness like Darth Vader's lightsaber through Luke's arm.

Catsby's eyes followed the darting red dot in the sky carefully, but he wasn't stupid. He made no attempt to jump off the door—water was no place for a cat. Hell, water was no place for a human being. If God had meant for us to swim, he'd have given us fins. That's why I was never a fan of Aquaman. He was unnatural, a heathen abomination. The silver lining to drowning at sea would be that I wouldn't live long enough to see an Aquaman movie.

After a few minutes of waving the laser pointer, it began to flicker. It soon died out completely. I hit it against the door a few times to get it to work again. No luck. We were doomed. I chucked the dead laser pointer into the sea.

"I guess that's it," I whispered in a horse voice to Catsby (or at least what I assumed a horse sounded like —I'd never heard one talk). "Maybe you won't live long enough to have babies. The more I think about it, I'd guess you're probably spayed or neutered, so that's a moot point. We're—"

I paused. A sound…in the distance.

"Did you hear that?"

Catsby looked at me like I was crazy. The sea drives you to madness, sure—that's well established in literature. Look at that poor chap in *Moby-Dick* who chased that whale around. Would he have chased an equally large elephant around? No, because the ocean does things to your mind. But I'd heard something. The sound of…wings flapping. I scanned the clouds in all directions. A bird? A plane?

"Judi Dench!"

The dragon descended through the clouds and cruised across the water toward us. Although ten larger than when I'd last seen her, she was still the same dragon I'd woken up with in the hotel bathtub. I've since learned that dragons grow at an incredibly fast pace, since they were originally engineered as weapons of war. You can't wait twenty years for your genetic weapon of mass destruction to mature.

Judi Dench flew low over us, and then turned around. On the second pass, she landed in the water with a terrible splash that nearly tipped Catsby off the door. I could see now that the dragon wasn't alone.

"Cordon!"

Judi Dench paddled close to us. Cordon, riding on her back, extended an arm. "Need a lift, lover boy?"

I gripped her hand and she pulled me aboard the dragon's back. "Hold on," I said. "We have to get Catsby."

"Catsby? But he's—"

I reached out for the cat, and he scrambled up my arms and into my lap. "This is Catsby," I said, petting the creature.

"He does look like him, doesn't he?"

"It's uncanny."

She paused. "You don't think that's..."

"Actually him? Stranger things have happened."

"You're right about that," she said. "Where were you guys headed, anyhow?"

"Nowhere fast," I said, trying to sound like a rebel. Instead I sounded like a dork. What else was new. "And you?"

"I found this dragon in one of Catsby's garages this week," Cordon said. "I'm supposed to be in California at another hot-dog eating competition next month. Until then, I don't know."

"Are you staying with Tucker and Miley?"

She shook her head. "Hadn't you heard? They left town."

"Say what?"

"What," she said.

"Thanks," I said. "So where did they go?"

"They just packed their bags and left town last night. Miley said they had two tickets to paradise. Wherever that is, I've no idea."

"Two tickets?" I said. "What about the kids?"

Cordon laughed. "I think they're kind of tired of being parents. Can you blame them?"

I nodded. "I was just starting out on a boat trip. Want to join me? I guess we'd have to find a new boat, but I heard the Mississippi River is nice this time of year. Just you, me, and Catsby."

The orange tabby meowed in recognition of his name.

"Forget the boat trip," Cordon said with a wicked smile. "Where we're going, we don't need boats."

She patted the dragon's neck. And with that, we flew off into the early morning sky. I didn't know what would happen between us, but there was a feeling in the air that anything was possible, because, hey, we were riding a freaking sweet-ass dragon. Plus, I still had Catsby's Rite-Aid card in my wallet. The future was wide open. Who knows? Maybe we'd even stop at a Shake Shack somewhere along the way.

And so Judi Dench's wings beat on...

ABOUT THE AUTHOR

Andrew Shaffer is the *New York Times* bestselling author of *Hope Never Dies: An Obama Biden Mystery* and the parody *Fifty Shames of Earl Grey*.

An Iowa native, Shaffer lives in Louisville, Kentucky with novelist Tiffany Reisz and two cats. One of the cats is sweet as pecan pie, but the other is a total asshole.

For more information:
www.andrewshaffer.com

facebook.com/authorandrewshaffer
instagram.com/andrew_shaffer

MORE BY ANDREW SHAFFER

IT'S
BEGINNING
TO LOOK
A LOT LIKE
F*CK THIS
ANDREW
SHAFFER

*It's Beginning to Look a Lot Like F*ck This* is an off-beat collection of Christmas parodies, essays, poems, and cartoons by *New York Times* bestselling humorist Andrew Shaffer.

"If you're looking for something tart to cut the holiday sweetness, Shaffer offers a naughty little treat." — *The Gazette*

CPSIA information can be obtained
at www.ICGtesting.com
Printed in the USA
LVHW031253230921
698566LV00013B/355

9 781949 769241